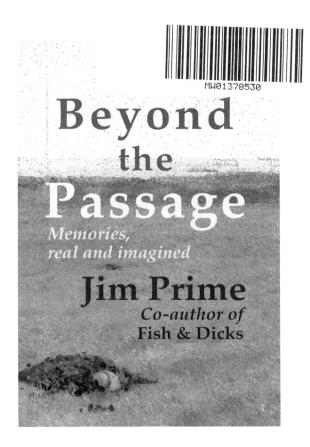

Whether he's writing about playing baseball in the fog, in a cow field, on an island in the Bay of Fundy; discussing murder at the kitchen table; being on the losing end in an argument with one's inner dialogue; or relating his personal struggle with pandemic pants; Jim manages to create characters and scenarios that the reader can easily identify with.

Ben Robicheau
author of *Two Ferries Out*

This book is a pleasure. After reading the first short story, I was hooked on a side of Jim's writing that I had not seen before: sensitive, nuanced, engaging. You don't have to have any connections to Jim's beloved Islands to become connected to them through these stories.

Andy Moir
Editor of *Passages*

Beyond the Passage: Memories, real and imagined
© 2023 Jim Prime

All rights reserved. No part of this book may be reproduced or transmitted in any form or by any means, electronic or mechanical, including photocopying, or by any information storage or retrieval system, without permission in writing from the publisher.

    The author expressly prohibits any entity from using this publication for purposes of training artificial intelligence (AI) technologies to generate text, including without limitation technologies that are capable of generating works in the same style or genre as this publication. The author reserves all rights to license uses of this work for generative AI training and development of machine learning language models.

Cover: Rebekah Wetmore
Editor: Andrew Wetmore

ISBN: 978-1-998149-25-4
First edition April, 2023
Schools edition September, 2023

2475 Perotte Road
Annapolis County, NS
B0S 1A0
moosehousepress.com
info@moosehousepress.com

We live and work in Mi'kma'ki, the ancestral and unceded territory of the Mi'kmaw People. This territory is covered by the "Treaties of Peace and Friendship" which Mi'kmaw and Wolastoqiyik (Maliseet) People first signed with the British Crown in 1725. The treaties did not deal with surrender of lands and resources but in fact recognized Mi'kmaq and Wolastoqiyik (Maliseet) title and established the rules for what was to be an ongoing relationship between nations. We are all Treaty people.

More Jim Prime books

From Moose House
Fish and Dicks: Case files from the Digby Neck and Islands Fish-Gutting Service and Detective Agency (with Ben Robicheau)
Ice Dreams: the 1972 Summit Series, 50 years on

From other publishers
Ted Williams Hit List (with Ted Williams)
Tales from the Boston Red Sox Dugout
More Tales from the Boston Red Sox Dugout
The Little Red (Sox) Book (with Bill Lee)
Red Sox Essentials
Baseball Eccentrics (with Bill Lee)
How Hockey Explains Canada (with Paul Henderson)
The Goal that United Canada
Amazing Tales from the 2004 Boston Red Sox Dugout
Ted Williams: a Tribute
Ted Williams: a Splendid Life
Fenway Park at 100
Fenway Saved
Tales from the Toronto Blue Jays Dugout
The Boston Red Sox World Series Encyclopedia
From the Babe to the Beards
Ted Williams, the Pursuit of Perfection
The Barber of Mud Creek
Boston Red Sox Killer Bs: Baseball's Best Outfield

Digby Neck and the Islands

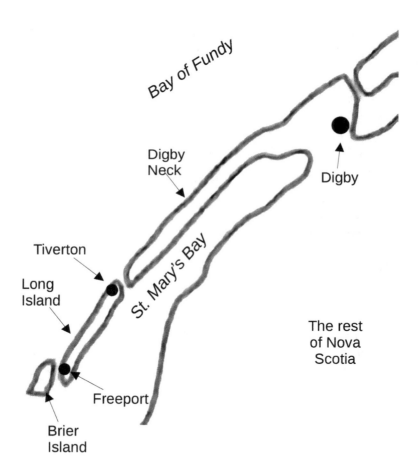

Preface

Beyond the Passage is a tribute to Long and Brier Islands, Nova Scotia. They will always be 'down home' to me. The reasons are countless, but allow me to count just a few.

First of all, the residents are the most resourceful, effortlessly funny, generous people that I have met in my lifetime.

Second, the islands are like Viagra for the imagination. A stent for writer's block. An elixir for the soul. They are so blessed with natural beauty that it's impossible for even lifelong residents to take it for granted. They have the most glorious sunsets in the known world and seascapes that somehow manage to fill you with longing *and* a sense of well-being at the same time.

The ever–changing ocean and the endless skies create a palette of brilliant blues that seem in sharper focus than their mainland counterparts. Lush green fields stretch toward the sea, often ending abruptly at a basalt cliff. Yellowed pastureland adorned with colourful field flowers slopes gently downward, where it gives way to picturesque inlets and coves.

In every direction the land inevitably meets the slapping waves of St. Mary's Bay or the Bay of Fundy. The first columns of stunted spruce trees bend away from the constant onshore wind, and behind them more upright specimens offer shelter and sustenance for various wildlife. Intoxicating smells of salt air, seaweed and fish mix with mown hay and fish. Fog horns and factory whistles compete with pounding surf and the screech of seagulls. These things conspire together to overload the senses. Even the much-maligned fog adds a dimension of intrigue and anticipation—but in moderation, of course, because it can quickly out-stay its welcome.

I feel sorry for those visitors who don't immediately fall in love with the islands. I don't understand them and never will. I question their good sense and good taste.

Some people suggest that bigger, or at least different, opportunities lie elsewhere, and I'd be accused of hypocrisy if I didn't agree. But whether you settle in downtown Toronto or rural Saskatchewan, the islands always draw you back home.

When I was growing up in Freeport, sports were important to me. They still are. I followed the NHL on our one TV station—CHSJ in Saint John—and squinted to make out the obscure figures skating across the screen filtered through a layer of snow and interference that required me to go outside and "turn the aerial" with a wrench that we'd permanently tethered to the metal pole that held it aloft.

Baseball was easier to access. We could find a Red Sox game on the radio even during the daytime. We also picked up the very best rock and roll stations from New York and Boston.

Our baseball field, which we dubbed Carmen Memorial Stadium after the farmer who owned the pasture, was heavily mined with cow pie IEDs (Incidental Excremental Deposits). Herring nets served as our backstop.

But I defy anyone to say they had more fun than we did. We played on a plateau of land with the Bay of Fundy beyond the first base line and St. Mary's Bay partially visible in deep, deep left field. It would be impossible to replicate the experience my friends and I had during those glorious summers anywhere else.

The imagination needs stimuli in order to thrive. It's true that it can survive and maybe even flourish in the most sterile environments. But when the imagination is so abundantly nourished by inspirational sights such as those that greet islanders every day, creativity of many kinds is nurtured.

In my case, the islands captured my imagination and held it hostage all my life. I feel blessed to have grown up with the people of Long Island, Brier Island, Westport, Freeport, Central Grove, and Tiverton. And honoured to write about these places that allow the imagination to run amok.

Not all the stories in this book are set on the islands, but most of them had their origins there: in my corner bedroom as the wind whipped the house during a fierce gale; or as I rowed out to Dartmouth Ledge with my California cousins in hopes of landing some tommy cod; or while standing at the cutting table at Connor Brothers' factory, skinning fish and absorbing the rich language and free-flowing discussions.

But it was my father's store that offered a master class in storytelling. When you opened the door to dad's store, your nostrils were immediately assaulted by a pungent mix of stale tobacco and Dustbane. A perpetual cloud of blue smoke swirled listlessly in the air, stinging the eyes and causing them to water. It was as if the ever-present Bay of Fundy fog had taken up residence inside as well.

When your eyes adjusted, you could make out several men seated on the repurposed church benches that occupied two walls of the square structure. The men were all leaning forward, elbows on knees. Some glanced up casually at those who entered the store; most didn't bother. These sturdy-teethed men clamped the stems of briar pipes so tightly that when they spoke their voices were accompanied by a series of Morse-code-like clicks. Unfiltered Export A cigarettes dangled precariously from chapped lips or between yellowed fingers.

Even as a teenager, I saw irony in the fact that the same men who now stretched and scratched and smoked and swore on these repurposed church pews once sat in them, stiff-backed and solemn, wearing their best Sunday suits. The name of God was seldom invoked here because my father wouldn't have allowed it, but if it was, it was in a different context entirely.

Curtis L. Prime's General Store was much more than a place to buy groceries and dry goods. It was where men went in the evening to gather and spread information. Subjects ranged from fish prices to weather forecasts to politics. In fact, the only subject never addressed from these pews was religion..

Women usually avoided the store because of the smoke that permeated their clothing. One exception was when new mothers brought their babies to be weighed on the same circa 1912 scale that weighed slabs of cheddar cheese or slices of bologna.

It was a sort of gentlemen's club and refuge from marital bliss, and was among the first places that the telephone operator at Central would call to locate someone in case of emergencies, the kind of place where tobacco and cigarettes were kept in open view behind the counter but feminine hygiene products were placed on the lower shelves out of sight so as not to offend the sensibilities of grizzled old fishermen.

Customers came and went, catching the flotsam and jetsam of conversations that had begun earlier and would finish much later. At noon hour and after school, ravenous kids from the nearby elementary and high schools arrived in packs of three and four. The younger ones headed directly to the candy case which sat atop the counter on the right as you entered. It featured a rounded glass surface against which every child's nose in the village had at one time or another been pressed. Inside was a vast array of candy bars and other dentist's nightmares, or perhaps dreams.

The teenagers were more sophisticated, ordering Nesbitt's Orange pop to wash down their Scotties chips.

This was where I'd come several times a day and the words and phrases and stories seeped into my brain and took up permanent residence. Many decades later they still resonate with me, especially whenever I return for a visit or run into a fellow islander.

Not all of these stories happened as described, and some didn't happen at all. But then, historical accuracy and hard facts were never reasons to listen in at the general store.

Grains of salt in very large shakers were required to swallow many of the stories back then. I suggest you have some at hand as you read these stories.

Jim Prime

To the people of Long and Brier Islands.
Your geography has made you resilient, independent, and proud.
Your geography has forced you to rely on one another.
Your geography has made you unique.
Don't ever change.

Disclaimer

The non-fiction stories in this volume shine an enhanced light on past days, throwing some people and events into sharp contrast and prominence which they may not have enjoyed at the time. These are stories, not court reporting, so there may be some divergence between the events as told and what other participants may remember.

The author has created the characters, conversations, and events in the fictional stories, and any resemblance in them to any actual person is unintended.

Beyond the Passage

Preface..5
The three letters..13
Jessie and Esther...40
The party game...45
Betrayal...49
The party line...56
The nudist colony..63
The cat burglar..74
Incident at The Beaverbrook...82
A duck's dilemma..90
The rights of spring..94
My internal monologue..101
The deer and the hunters..112
No second chances at first pitches...114
The Phantom of Fenway...122
The magic baseball card..131
Mary and Harry's Obituaries..137
Amethyst summer..144
Finally, Finley..162
The perfect ending...170
Acknowledgements...179
About the author...183

Note:

"The Magic Baseball Card" has appeared in several collections of short stories, including *Swinging Below A Star* (Strategies series anthology), published by Nelson Canada.

Jim Prime

The three letters

1

Gertrude Robbins lived in a weathered, tree-shrouded house at the top of the grassy lane that ran past our home in Freeport, Nova Scotia. The village is located at the tip of Long Island, and years of exposure to salt-laden onshore winds, coupled with intermittent and extended stretches of fog and sun, had rendered her two-story dwelling completely devoid of paint. Spring gales and fall hurricanes had loosened many roof shingles and lifted several more, and the branches of three ancient chestnut trees lay heavily on the peak, softening its symmetry. Overgrown rose bushes bordering the outer wall had knitted into a tangled hedge and encroached on the worn wooden steps that led up to the front door.

I had long since convinced my six-year-old self that old Miss Robbins was a witch, my knowledge of witches admittedly limited to illustrations in my small library of Little Golden books, *Illustrated Fairy Tales*, and the Classic Comics Junior version of Hansel and Gretel. I formed this opinion during my first conscious encounter with her.

It was a Saturday morning in early spring and my father was taking me trout fishing in the small brook that served as the property line some hundred yards beyond the old woman's house. I was riding piggyback, my arms around dad's neck, when we saw her beside the front step, watering her geraniums.

My father called her name and greeted her warmly, complimenting her on her flowers. When she looked around, her appearance startled me so much that I buried my face in my father's neck.

Jim Prime

She wore an olive-coloured shawl and a jet black bonnet. Her face was wrinkled and very white. Her mouth was lop-sided and hung open in what I saw as a toothless grin. But the telltale sign, the accessory that left no doubt in my mind, was one that no self-respecting witch would be without, a dark wart on her left cheek.

To my amazement, my father ignored all of these obvious warning signs. He asked how she was and she struggled to answer, her words garbled. I heard phrases like "mild stroke" and "feeling a bit better."

"Say hello to our neighbour, Miss Robbins," my father said.

I peeked out but couldn't speak.

"Hello, child," she said with difficulty. "That's alright. We'll meet and talk some other time."

It sounded to me like a threat.

My father said goodbye and she mumbled something back. I watched over my shoulder as she put down the watering can and picked up a broom to sweep the rickety steps. I shivered as I contemplated what other uses she made of the broom late at night when the moon was high in the sky.

It was the briefest of encounters but one that left a vivid and lasting impression. She fit all the criteria for being a witch as I understood them.

As we continued to the brook, I asked my father if Miss Robbins had a family and he said, no, that she was a spinster. The word rang a bell. Hadn't Rumpelstiltskin been a spinster? An evil creature who spun straw into gold? My mind fought to make a connection.

Each time I saw her after that, a chill passed through me. Whenever we had reason to pass by her place she was framed in the front window, sitting in a rocking chair, knitting items of clothing that I doubted would ever be worn. I watched as her fingers guided the long needles with great speed, creating a frenzy of tiny stabbing motions, and although I could hear nothing, I imagined clicking sounds accompanied by cackling.

In the year that followed, I was occasionally required to go to her door to deliver groceries and the *Star Weekly* from my father's corner store. The first time I entered the house my senses were overwhelmed by an odour completely foreign to me. It was a stale smell, not exactly dirty but unpleasant, a heady mix of soured milk, lavender and old age that had been left to marinate over many years.

I left the groceries inside the door and fled. I broke into a run and didn't slow until I reached our yard and bounded up the back door steps.

The foul odour seemed to cling to me long after I left, like a living thing that had invaded my nostrils and taken up residence. I found it hard to shake the notion that the spirit of this old woman had somehow entered me and was lying there—incubating, waiting for just the right moment to strike.

My father wasn't happy when I told him that I hadn't waited to speak with Miss Robbins. He called it rude and disrespectful and said he was disappointed in me. He didn't ask me to deliver to her again for several weeks.

At first I was pleased, but as time passed, the rebuke continued to sting and I desperately wanted to redeem myself in his eyes.

One warm summer evening in August my father once again called on me to carry out the perilous mission of bringing sustenance to the probable witch. He repeated the usual instructions: I was to knock twice and, if there was no answer, enter and take the groceries to the kitchen immediately on my right, placing them on the table. I was then told to go to the parlour. If Miss Robbins was awake, I was to greet her and tell her that her groceries had been delivered. If she was asleep, I was to leave, making sure that I latched the door quietly behind me.

"She's in poor health," he added, "and her memory isn't sharp."

On all previous visits, she had been asleep and I was able to complete my task without confronting the sorceress.

I carried the large paper bag of foodstuffs the quarter mile from the store to her home, cutting across the school property to save time. I knocked on the door and waited, and when there was no reply knocked again.

There was still no response, so I turned the knob and pushed gently. When the door resisted, I pushed harder and it swung open

Jim Prime

with a long squeak of protest. I went in, moved mechanically to the right, and placed the bag at the centre of the sturdy kitchen table.

I moved down the short hallway that led to the parlour and looked in. The air was warm and oppressive and I looked around and noticed that all the windows were closed tightly, faded lace curtains pulled across all but the one where she sat. The resultant shadows turned the living room into a realm of indistinct forms and ghoulish colours. The ancient chesterfield was of faded purple velvet, yellowed doilies draped over the arms and back.

When my eyes finally adjusted to the dim light I could see that the furniture was heavy, black and ornate. Bookcases and cabinets supported equally-ornate picture frames in which unsmiling people in shapeless suits and frumpy dresses stared at me as if to say I was not welcome here.

I stared at Miss Robbins silhouette against the window and jumped slightly when I saw her move. She was awake.

She looked up from her knitting and motioned with a withered finger for me to come nearer. I did so reluctantly. Up close, her face showed an unhealthy pallor and the wrinkles that I remembered so vividly from our first meeting had deepened.

But her face was serene, and I was surprised that there was no wart, as I had remembered, just a small discoloration that might have been a freckle. Her mouth still hung slightly agape as if she were always about to speak, but her smile was not the crooked grin I had remembered, nor was it toothless. Her teeth were most likely false, but they were present and accounted for.

When she did speak her voice was as thin as the grey strands of hair that protruded from beneath her black bonnet, but there was no slurring. "Thank you, Charles. You were always a good boy."

"It's Danny," I said. "Danny Titus. Charles is my dad."

She stared at me, momentarily annoyed, and then her face softened. "Of course it is, child. You'll have to forgive a foolish old woman. My memory isn't what it once was."

Her eyes were rheumy and she dabbed at them with the sleeve of her sweater. She thanked me for the groceries and told me to take a quarter from the tin box on the warming closet of the Iron

Beyond the Passage

Duke stove on the way out.

As I passed back through the hallway that led to the entrance, I heard her say, "Please thank your mother for the wonderful gift."

I stopped and hesitated for a moment before managing a squeaky, "Pardon me?"

There was no reply, and when I looked around the corner, her head was lowered, her brow furrowed in total concentration on her knitting.

Outside, the cool evening air struck my face and I greedily gulped it in, letting it wash over me. As I started down the lane toward home, I looked back and saw Miss Robbins sitting at the window, her hands moving rhythmically, expertly, as the knitting needles glinted and danced in the setting sun.

This time I didn't run. I walked quickly but deliberately, while doing my best to look casual.

My mother was taking sheets and pillow cases from the clothesline, carefully folding them before placing them in the laundry basket. As she deposited the clothespins in her apron pocket, she heard my feet on the stairs and called my name. I responded with a small wave and hurried into the house, the screen door clanging shut in my wake.

My dog Chum greeted me, tail wagging, but I rushed past him and went straight to the bathroom. I placed my hands on either side of the sink and stared into the mirror, fighting to catch my breath. I turned on the tap and splashed cold water on my face, rubbing it through my hair.

I decided to take a bath, careful to follow our family's self-imposed summer water ration policy. Our water was the coldest, softest, and purest that I ever tasted, but during July and August our shallow dug well regularly ran dry. I ran just enough water to cover my legs, mixing cold and hot with a practised touch, then settled back in the shallow water and scrubbed myself clean with soap and a washcloth.

2

At breakfast next morning, my mom and dad were discussing a recent incident involving the ferry that connected Long Island to the mainland. Apparently the ferry had lost its power midway across Petite Passage and the powerful tides had carried it past Balancing Rock before they managed to get the engine restarted. The Department of Transportation had been down the previous day to conduct an inquiry and restore public confidence in the service.

Finally, dad glanced up at the clock and said he'd better get going. The store was only a short walk but it was almost 9:00, opening time.

When he'd left, my mother finished the last of her coffee, then moved to the sink and began washing dishes as I ate my cereal. The radio was playing a soap jingle and she was humming along.

I tried to sound as nonchalant as possible. "Mom, how old would Miss Robbins be?"

My mother looked up, placed a plate in the drying rack, and cocked her head slightly to one side. "Hmmm. Well, she must be in her late seventies I would think...No, no, I'm telling a fib. She's more than that. I remember your father saying that she went to school with your grandfather. Let's see, that would have been before the turn of the century, so she must have been born around 1890 or so. So, what's that make? Oh, about 80 I guess."

"She looks older," I said.

She chuckled. "Well some people just age differently, I guess."

She seemed to be waiting for a follow-up question and when none came she said, "Why are you asking?"

"Oh, nothing. I delivered her groceries last night."

"Yes, well, I hope you were polite."

"I was."

"Good."

"She's kind of scary. Her mouth hardly moves when she talks."

"Yes, well that doesn't matter, does it?"

"I guess not. Where'd she come from, anyway?"

"I think she was born here. Robbins have been here as long as the village, along with the Primes, Thurbers, Haineses, and Tituses. I do know that her mother and father are lying side by side in the Riverside Cemetery."

Beyond the Passage

"Was she ever married?"

"I don't think so. She still has her maiden name. Your father could tell you more about her."

"He told me she was a spinster."

"Well, there you go."

I quickly deduced that spinster had nothing to do with spinning wheels and evil imps. "She said to thank you for the gift."

"What?"

"She said to thank you for the wonderful gift."

"What gift? I didn't give her any gift. Just a card after her stroke. I've probably only spoken with her a half dozen times in the last two years. She's confused."

"I guess," I said.

"Listen, I have errands to run. If you're so interested in Gertrude —that's her first name—ask your father, or maybe Will Thurber around the cove. He's about the oldest person on the island and he's blessed with a marvellous memory. Loves to talk, too."

"Okay," I said and retreated to my bedroom where I half-heartedly sorted through my pile of Superman comics, picked out an old favourite and sprawled on the bed.

I began reading, but couldn't concentrate and tossed it aside. Suddenly I wanted to find out everything I could about the lady who had appeared so often in my dreams and nightmares.

My mother shouted goodbye and said she'd be back around noon. I went outside and stared for a long moment at the Robbins place, then jumped on my bike. Chum barked loudly, begging to come along, then lay down and whimpered when I told him to stay. I made a note to take him for a walk when I got back.

Our house was located at the head of the horseshoe-shaped cove that split the village in half. I turned left at the bottom of the lane and headed down the dirt road that hugged the water. The damp morning air felt good against my skin as I pumped the pedals over the newly-graded gravel.

The tide was advancing across the flats, flooding the surface and carrying with it an assortment of microscopic lifeforms. Small clusters of gulls and snipes edged the water, making strategic ad

19

Jim Prime

vances and retreats as they gorged themselves on the delicacies.

Ten minutes later I turned my bike onto the government wharf and braked. Cape Islanders were lined up stern to bow on both sides of the wooden structure, two deep in some places. Fishermen were busy repairing gear and fine-tuning engines.

I spotted three men idling at the end of the wharf and walked my bike toward them. The two younger men were standing, one smoking a cigarette, the other rolling one. They were listening intently to the third man, perched like a seagull on a tarred wooden piling, waving his lit pipe about as he spoke. I'd only met him once before but I knew that the old man was Will Thurber.

The three hadn't noticed me approach and I waited patiently as Will spun a story about the time he caught so many haddock that he had to pitch some overboard for fear of sinking. When he had finished he returned the pipe to his mouth and clenched it tightly between his teeth, his eyes dancing. The two men shook their heads, deciding if he was pulling their legs.

During the momentary pause, I took the opportunity to speak. "Hello, Mr. Thurber."

He looked up and squinted at me, blocking the sun from his eyes with his gnarled hand. He wore a flat wool cap, overalls and rubber boots. The skin on his face was pink and smooth with small patches of white. It looked paper thin.

He considered me for a moment and then spoke, "Well, I know you're a Titus so you gotta be Charles' boy."

"Yes, Daniel. Danny."

"Acourse you are! Well, how are you, Daniel?"

"Pretty good. I was wondering if I could ask you some things." Will nodded at the other two and they drifted away to continue their speculation in peace.

When they had left, Will said, "Fire away, son."

"My mother said that you have a good memory."

"I do have that. I can look out toward that passage and remember them four masters that used to go back and forth through there regular as clockwork. This place was a beehive in them days."

"It's about an old lady I deliver groceries to."

Beyond the Passage

"Well there ain't many people on these islands I haven't had dealin's with across my life."

"It's Miss Robbins. Her first name is—"

"Oh, Gertrude. Acourse I know Gertrude. She's a bit younger but we was in school together. Well, well. Haven't seen Gert in a while. How'd you find her?"

"Pretty good, I guess. She does a lot of knitting."

Will chuckled. "Always did. Back in the Great War, she knitted all manner of scarves and socks and long johns for the men overseas. Even organized a knitting circle at the church vestry. Most of 'em had husbands overseas, ya see. But Gertrude did it out of the goodness of her heart."

"Were you in the war?"

Someone shouted up from a boat. "Hey Will, make yourself useful."

Will moved to a nearby wharf cleat, undid the clove hitch that secured the bow line and tossed it to a crew member. He moved to the stern line and repeated the operation. The man yelled thanks and used a long-handled gaff to push the boat away from the side. The idling engine let out a full-throated roar and the boat moved smoothly toward the open water beyond the breakwater, leaving a barely discernible wake. A scattering of seagulls followed the boat at a respectful distance. Other boats followed suit until only those whose keels were still resting on the sandy bottom above the rising tide were left.

When the sound of engines faded, Will said, "No, never in the war. Had TB just before it started. Spent the first two years in the San up to Kentville. Tried to join up after I recovered, but I was the skin of a nightmare by then. Went to the recruiting office in Digby and they took one look at me and told me to go home. Waited a few weeks, then went to Yarmouth and tried again.

"Got as far as the physical that time but that was it. I joined the home guard...that's what they called it. Mostly women who went to work in the factories to keep 'em goin'. I worked alongside of 'em, taught 'em how to gut and skin and fillet. Wasn't long afore they was faster'n I was. I helped out around the village where I could,

Jim Prime

doin' odd jobs for them that was left behind. Every time someone from these islands was reported killed or injured in action, it was like bein' stuck with a bayonet. When Penny got that telegram in late spring, 1917 sayin' that your grandfather was missin' in action...hardest time of my life."

"You knew my grandfather?" I said. I had been so intent on learning about Gertrude, I'd given no thought to the likelihood that my own grandfather was a contemporary.

"Knew him? Why we was closer 'n two peas in a pod, me and Matthew Titus. He was my best friend. I sat with Penny pretty well every night for three weeks, drinkin' coffee and sayin' prayers. News durin' the war was terrible slow comin'. She had the young one—your father—to tend to on top of it all. He was just a toddler."

He paused to draw a dirty handkerchief from his overalls and blew his nose loudly, wiping it several times before jamming it back in a pocket. "Then we got word he was alive, and we both cried like babies, me and Penny. Those devils had gassed the bunch of em at Vimy Ridge, in March. Chlorine gas. Dirty buggers. He'd been evacuated to a French hospital to recover."

My grandfather had died years before I was born, but I'd spent many rainy afternoons looking through photo albums with black and white pictures of him in uniform, with school mates, staring out from wedding pictures alongside grammie, and with various nameless people. There were also newer family pictures with my father at picnics, and one of them standing alongside a deer that had been strung up in a barn to bleed. Grampie was cradling a rifle and dad looked like he'd rather be someplace else.

"The things we used to get up to, Matt 'n me," said Will. "High old times. Shouldn't tell you this but one time on a dare we stole a punt from old Mr. Ruggles and went for a row to Westport. It was windy and we ran aground on the shoal by Gull Rock and almost drowned. Had to hang onto the bell buoy till help came 'bout an hour later. Damn thing kept clanging, almost deafened us both."

He stuck his fingers in both ears and dug at them vigorously. "I can still hear that cussed ringing some days. Anyways, guess who rescued us? Old Mr. Ruggles hisself. Never said a word more about

Beyond the Passage

it even though his punt sank. We coulda been in a lot of trouble with our parents. Nice feller Mr. Ruggles—used to wink at us every time he saw us after that."

He laughed silently and his whole body shook.

"What did Miss Robbins look like back then?" I asked.

"Oh, she was awful pretty, had a little beauty mark right here." He pointed to his left cheek. "Just like them silent film stars, Lillian Gish and Mary Pickford and them. 'Cept hers weren't pasted on. The other girls was some jealous."

"She must have had a lot of boyfriends."

Will's eyes crinkled. "No, no, not Gertie. They was a few buzzin' round her for a while, myself included, if I'm honest."He shook his head. "No one dared go near her."

"Why not?"

"Her mother and father were strict Baptists, ya see, the kind that thought most everything was a sin. God himself knows how they ever got together—or how they ever figured out how to make a baby. Musta been the second virgin birth, far as I can tell. School and church, that's the only time Gertrude spent any time with boys. We used to tease her something wicked, me and your grampie, called her Gert the flirt or Flirty Gertie, just to get her goat. She pretended to be mad but I think she liked it."

The tide was nearly high and the last few boats had floated free of the bottom. We turned to watch as more engines roared to life and lines were cast off. Soon we were alone on the wharf.

Will took a matchbox from his pocket, and relit his pipe, taking several long draws before tossing the spent match into the water. He leaned forward, elbows on knees. "Gert was born and raised in that same house she's rattlin' around in today, you know," he said, shaking his head. "Like servin' a life sentence in that there Dorchester Penitentiary."

I suddenly felt sorry for the woman I had been convinced was a witch.

"She never had nothing pretty to wear. Family was no worse off than any of us, neither. She always looked neat and clean. A natural beauty, you'd call her. She was at her friend's birthday party one

23

Jim Prime

time—they only let her go because there was no boys invited. Anyways, one of the girls got hold of some lipstick and they was all tryin' it on. When her father come to pick her up he saw it on her and went crazy right there in front of everyone. Found out later they scrubbed her face with lye soap."

He grew quiet for a while as if trying to organize his thoughts.

"Never lost her spirit though, God bless her," he finally said. "She was quiet but she had lots a gumption. She'd stop at her friend Alida's on the way to school sometimes and Alida would give her a few things to spruce her up a bit. A ribbon for her hair, maybe, or a barrette or a necklace. Always looked nice. Then she'd change back after school before she went home."

"Couldn't anybody help her?"

"Wasn't like it is nowadays. They didn't beat her or nothing, not that I know of, anyways. It was more what you call pickin' at her all the time. Nothin' she did was right. They was always shamin' her, callin' her Jezebel, and worse names too. There wasn't a single photograph taken of her; leastways none that I know of. If she even glanced in her mirror they called her prideful. Finally removed it from her bedroom altogether, or so they say. Didn't stop her from brushing that long hair till it shined—people was always complimentin' her on that hair of hers. Well, one day she comes to school and it's all cut off short. Her mother did it herself. Said vanity was a sin. Dances was a sin. Talkin' to boys was a sin. Far as I can see, what they did to that poor girl was a sin."

I heard the noon whistle blow at the fish factory and knew my mom would be wondering where I was. "Well, thanks, Mr. Thurber. I better get back home."

"Come visit agin some time, young feller. I knew I recognized you. You're the spittin' image of your dad, except for that red hair of yours."

"My dad says he left me out in the rain too long one day and it rusted," I said, mounting my bike.

Will smiled. "Most likely that's it, boy. You know, I still miss your granddad every day, and that's the truth. He died too soon. That goddamn gas weakened his lungs, ya see. And poor Penny joined

Beyond the Passage

him, what...about four, five years ago? You remember her, son?"

"A bit. I remember she was nice and smelled like soap. She had pictures of Grampie on the wall. He was holding a big fish in one of them."

"I was there when he caught that fish," he said. "Biggest halibut I ever saw."

I gave him a final wave and peddled toward home.

3

The years passed and thoughts of Miss Robbins all but faded from my mind. There were still occasional trips to her house to deliver groceries, but I no longer thought she was a witch. In fact, I was ashamed of those childish notions.

My friends and I played pond hockey and organized massive snowball fights in the winters, but the summers were the best. We carved out a baseball diamond in the hayfield across the brook and played until it was too dark to see the ball. We picked pennywinkles and sold them to Mr. Melanson, who said he'd take all we could bring him. We took BB guns to the beach, where we tried and failed to shoot snipes. We caught eels and sold them to the paving crew from the French Shore. We played cowboys and Indians on the ridge that overlooked the Bay of Fundy on one side and St. Mary's Bay on the other.

One Saturday, just a few weeks after my thirteenth birthday, I was walking home from Beautiful Cove, where my best friend Gary and I had been skipping beach rocks and searching for amethyst to sell to tourists. As I passed my father's store, he waved me in and asked if I could make a delivery. It was payday at the factory and inside the store was a haze of smoke as the men bought their weekly groceries and exchanged stories.

I said sure and dad gave me a large bag of groceries. "Take these to Miss Robbins, please. And mind your manners!" He grinned, letting me know he was kidding.

"Okay, dad," I said and grinned back, but I must have sounded less than enthusiastic.

Jim Prime

"You don't mind, do you, Danny?" he said. "She's a nice old lady. She's had a hard life. She's always been good to us."

"Whataya mean?"

"Oh, she was nice to all the kids. But she seemed to like me. Knit mittens for me every winter. She even loaned me some money to help start this store. Told me not to tell a soul."

A customer interrupted to ask him for some Export As and I took the groceries and walked the familiar route to Miss Robbins' place.

I knocked on the old lady's door and then walked in and put the groceries on the kitchen table just as I'd done before.

When I went into the parlour, Miss Robbins greeted me warmly. "I saw you coming across the lawn, Charles. You look more like your father every day, I swear. You here for some cookies?"

I tried to correct her but she ignored me.

"I think there's some in the jar on the kitchen counter. You know where it is. Go help yourself. You going to climb the tree again today?"

I didn't know what to say. She had gone too far to correct her now without embarrassment. "Not today, ma'am, got to get home."

"Course you do. Penny'll be worried. You go run along, now. Don't forget them cookies."

"I won't," I said and retreated to the kitchen. I glanced at the counter and spotted a large blue ceramic cookie jar in the far corner. It had a smiley clown face painted on it. I hesitated, then went over and lifted the lid.

As I suspected, there were no cookies, only a few old letters tied neatly together with a length of yarn. The one on top had a strange stamp that caught my attention.

I replaced the lid, took several steps toward the door and paused. I went back to the cookie jar, opened the lid, took the letters and carefully put them inside my jacket and zipped it up before hurrying outside.

Miss Robbins waved to me from the window as I headed down the lane. I returned an awkward wave, not wanting the letters to slip from beneath my windbreaker.

Beyond the Passage

When I got to the house I went to my bedroom and closed the door. I placed the thin packet on my dresser and carefully undid the knot.

There were three envelopes. I placed them side by side on the dresser and stared at them

All three were discoloured by time. One bore two halfpenny stamps bearing the likeness of King George V and was addressed to Miss Gertrude Robbins, Freeport, NS, Canada. There was no return address. I looked closer at the blurred postmark circles and could make out the word Bramshot, UK.

The next envelope, also addressed to Gertrude, had two French stamps and a return address that said, Hôpital 2, Eyreaux, Eure.

The writing on the third letter was flowing and elegant, obviously a woman's hand. It was addressed to Pvt. Matthew Titus, C/O Camp Debert, Debert, NS. It had no return address and no postmark. It had never been sent.

I pulled a chair to me and sat down and then arranged the envelopes from my grandfather by date and carefully extracted the first letter.

> *April 15, 1916.*
> *Dear Gertie,*
> *Your letter and package of Dec. 5, 1915 sent to me in Debert finally caught up with me in south of England where me and my pals are awaiting orders. Can't say more. Thanks so much for the socks. I'm sure they'll soon come in handy.*
> *I want you to know that I regret what happened. My fault, not yours. Hope you are well and able to get out and about more. Also hope our friendship can resume as before.*
> *Sincerely,*
> *Matthew*

I refolded the brittle letter, slid it into the envelope and opened the second.

Jim Prime

April 30, 1916
Dear Gert,
I'm sure that by now you've heard the news that Penny is expecting. It's a complete surprise but wonderful news and it's helping me get through the long days here. I am currently in hospital in southern France, having been evacuated here after a poison gas attack in Vimy. I'm luckier than most. The lads at the front of our charge got the brunt of it. I still have breathing problems. Not sure what the future holds but expect to be mustered out and sent home.

Hope you can be happy for Penny and me. You are such a wonderful gal and I wish only the best for you. I pray that your home situation has become more tolerable. Penny says you've gone to NB to help out relatives there. Glad to hear it. Say hi to Will if you see him before me and tell him to stay out of trouble (ha-ha).
Your friend,
Matthew

I returned it to the envelope, picked up the third envelope and regarded it nervously before opening it and extracting a single neatly folded page.

May 23, 1916
My dearest Matthew,
I hope you are well and far from the terrible battles I read about in the paper. This is a very difficult letter to write and I considered not doing so but felt you have a right to know. I have recently discovered that I am with child. I tell you this only because I think you deserve to know and not because I have any expectations of you. Mother and father have arranged to send me away to mother's sister's home in Saint John while my uncle Mordechai is serving God through his ministry to Canadian soldiers in England. I will await the baby's arrival there and remain during my lying in period,

28

Beyond the Passage

and maybe longer. I will then put him or her up for adoption. It is best for everyone. Please don't worry. I am fine and strong and will ensure that the child – our child – finds a good home. The last thing I wish to do is cause hurt to you and dear Penny.
With affection,
Gertrude
P.S. I realize the folly of our actions, but want you to know that I don't regret it. Perhaps I should. Perhaps, as my parents say, I am not a good Christian and my soul is in peril, but I'm not sorry.

Three letters. Two from my grandfather to Gertrude Robbins and one from Gertrude to my grandfather, addressed and stamped but never sent.

4

I leaned back in the chair, trying to grasp the meaning of this when my eye drifted to something protruding from the un-mailed letter. I pulled it out and saw that it was a lock of auburn hair tied up in white ribbon.

I thought about the events the rest of the day and long into the evening until finally surrendering to a fitful sleep. I woke early the next morning and sat at the breakfast table, speaking only when spoken to. I stole long looks at my father as he talked with mom, carefully studying his face.

After lunch I went up to our attic and rummaged around until I found the cardboard box containing the family photo albums. Some were from my mother's family in Tiverton and some from dad's side. I finally found the one I was looking for and opened it, flipping the pages until I found the picture that had stuck in my mind. It was of the Church sewing circle, marked December, 1915.

I removed the photo, folded a nearby piece of cardboard around it and put it in my pocket. Once downstairs, I rushed out to my bike and rode as fast as I could to the government wharf, where I hoped

Jim Prime

I'd find Will. When I got there, there was no sign of him.

I walked down the wharf and peered over the side. He was sitting in his rowboat, baling water with a wooden scoop. I called his name and he waved for me to come down. I descended the rusted iron ladder and jumped aboard the boat.

"Hey, Daniel. Take a seat there on that thwart."

He stopped baling and sat opposite me at the bow. "Just getting rid of some rain water. Boats as tight as a frog's ass, excuse my French, but it rained overnight. What brings you down here again so soon?"

"I had another question about Gertrude. You said she started up a sewing circle to darn socks and things for the soldiers."

"She sure did. She got it goin'."

I carefully pulled the picture from my jacket pocket, unfolded the cardboard, and handed it to him. He wiped his hands on his overalls several times and grasped it by the edge.

"What's this?"

"It's a picture of that sewing circle. My grammie was in it, too. That's her on the far left."

"So it is."

"But where's Gertrude?"

Will held the picture close to his eyes, examining the faces of the twelve women sitting around a circular table, darning needles in hand, staring at the camera.

"What year's this?" he said.

I pointed to the date written on the back.

"December, 1916."

"Oh, that'd be why," he said. "About the one and only time I figure Gertrude was off this island was durin' the war. Oh she may have been to a couple of Missionary Society do's to Digby with her mother, but that weren't no holiday for her. Not long after the war broke out, she went to stay with her mother's sister over to Saint John, kept her company while her husband was overseas. He was a minister, I think. Quite a number of women left the island to wait out the war with relatives up the line. Just packed up their belongings and moved. Some of their husbands was stationed in Halifax

30

Beyond the Passage

or Debert before they went overseas. I tended to some of their houses while they was gone. Had to do something to be useful. That'd be why she ain't there."

He pointed to the picture of my grandmother.

"Course your grammie left, too, a few months later. Found out she was pregnant with your father three or four months after Matthew shipped out, that was in December, 1915. She was some excited, told everyone in the village she was going to have a baby. I remember some of the old gossips sayin' as how it was temptin' fate to talk about it, bad luck, and all them old wives' tales, but she didn't care. Her and Matthew thought they couldn't have kids, ya see. They'd bin tryin' for a while, Matthew told me."

He handed the photo back to me. "I told her I'd be round to help her out as her time got near, but she said thanks but no, she was goin' to go to Halifax to be close to the hospital. Made sense, stayed with some relative or other down there. Poor Matthew never saw your father till he was a couple of years old. They moved him from that French hospital to England and finally shipped him home to Halifax. They'd just opened Camp Hill Hospital so he was with other soldiers. The day he got back here everyone in the village turned out to greet him up at the IOOF Hall. He was always popular, big strong handsome fella."

He paused and winked. "Like me. People from Westport and Tiverton come, too. People was desperate for some good news for a change."

He looked out across the water and when he looked back his face had darkened. "I hardly recognized him at first. Looked like an old man. Turns out he had what they used to call shell shock, too. They didn't talk about that much in them days. Afraid of being called yellow, what they called malingerers. Penny walked up to him and put her hand on his face. Then she handed him his son and I was scared to death he might drop him, that's how weak he was. But he didn't, he held him just fine, big smile on his face. He kissed your dad right on the mouth and Charles made a funny face and wiped it off. The people all laughed and clapped and cheered and there wasn't a dry eye anywhere. Matthew waved but he didn't

Jim Prime

make no speech. We had to help him into his house. Everyone brought food."

"What about Gertrude?"

"She stayed in Saint John till the end of the war. I remember thinking, 'Well at least this war got old Gert away from that prison for a spell.' I hoped she'd stay away—woulda been the best thing for her. But she came back. Moved right back into that house with Orson and Violet. Looked after 'em till they died, God bless her Christian soul, coupla weeks apart in the early 1920s."

"She was young. Why didn't she move away after that?"

"God knows. Folks are funny. After a while they kinda get comfortable in their misery, I guess. Or don't know enough about life to know what they're missin'. She did go out a bit more. School concerts and things like that. Even taught Sunday school as I recall. And volunteered at the school."

I tried to picture old Miss Robbins teaching Sunday school but the image failed to form in my mind.

That evening after supper, dad had returned to the store and mom was reading in the sunporch. I took the letters from my sock drawer, quietly slipped out of the house and walked up the lane.

Gertude was not in the window. Without knocking, I opened the door and moved quickly to the kitchen, where I opened the cookie jar and put the letters back.

As I was replacing the lid, Gertrude came into the kitchen and saw me. "Are you after more of my cookies, young man?" she asked playfully. I decided it was time to discover the truth.

"There are no cookies," I said. She looked at me quizzically. "I took your letters. I read them."

The effect on her was immediate and frightening. Suddenly her knees seemed unable to support her and she pitched forward. She clutched at the back of a chair, which broke her fall long enough for me to rush to her side. Her face was drained of the little colour she had.

I helped her into the parlour and sat her down on the chesterfield, then went and got a glass of cold water from the kitchen. I held the glass as she took some tentative sips and soon her colour

Beyond the Passage

had returned.

"How much do you know?" she said.

"I know about you and Matthew...you and grampie," I said gently. "I know you got sent away and had the baby. I know you wrote a letter to him and never mailed it. I know you put your child up for adoption. That's...that's it."

When I offered her more water, she clutched the glass with both hands and took a long drink. "Sit down on the hassock, Danny, and I'll tell you everything. These are things that most boys your age wouldn't understand, but I have no choice now."

She took a deep breath and cleared her throat. At first the words came haltingly but soon the floodgates opened and the story poured out, as if she had played it over in her mind a thousand times.

"I was...I was a lonely girl. The only friends I had were in school and church and...and I seldom saw them except in those places. You see, Daniel, my mother and father were very...religious people. They believed that the devil was all around us. They...they weren't very affectionate...to each other, or to me. There were no hugs, no kisses. We used to have a barn and I remember one day while he was milking the cow my father found a litter of yellow kittens in the hay. When he came in the house, he told mother about them and said he would get rid of them. I went out to the barn and took one and hid with it up in the hay loft. I watched through a crack as he put the rest in a burlap bag. When he went outside I followed him down to the cove and saw him put a large rock in the bag and throw it into the water. That's the kind of man he was.

"Anyway, Matthew...that is, your grandfather was always nice to me in school, he and Will Thurber. They made me feel normal, attractive even. Some of the girls were okay too, but your grandfather was special. The girls all had crushes on him.

"When we got older and left school, I only saw him now and then, but when I did, he always made a fuss about me and made me laugh. Then he started goin' out with your grandmother, Penny Andrews she was then, from up in Tiverton. Within a few months, they ended up getting married. When I heard about it, I remember

Jim Prime

feeling empty. I'm not sure why, we were never more than friends.

"Penny joined our church and we used to talk after the service sometimes over coffee. Just small talk. She mentioned that she and Matt were trying to have a baby. I never brought the subject up, but every once in a while, she'd open up about it. She was worried that maybe they couldn't have children. Matt even went to the doctor to see if there was a problem but Dr. Thomas assured him that there wasn't.

"Then the war came.

"Everyone got all fired up and patriotic and the boys all wanted to enlist. They thought it'd be an adventure. Thought it'd all be over in a matter of weeks. I was down at the fish factory one day to pick up some fresh haddock for dinner and along came Matthew, just back from fishing. We walked home together and he told me he had enlisted and would be leaving in a week or so. For some reason, I started crying. Just like that. I cried and cried and couldn't stop. It was like everything had been building up, you know, and it all came out at once.

"He felt bad for me. I was a mess. I couldn't go home looking like that. We walked up to the ridge and sat in the grass and looked down at the village. He put his arm around me, just to comfort me...I know it's hard to understand but...one thing led to another and...well...I kissed him and he kissed me back. And then one thing led to another and we just couldn't stop...

"Anyways, it was just one of those things, and afterwards we walked home and barely said a word. He gave me a little hug when we parted and we went our separate ways. I didn't lay eyes on him again till after the war.

"He was called up right after that. Sent to Camp Debert outside of Truro, for training.

"Three months later, I knew I was pregnant. Mother noticed it before I did, thought I had gained some weight at first. Then she knew. I had no idea, none whatsoever. When my father found out he was so furious that I think even mother was afraid of what he might do.

"The next few weeks were just awful. They locked me in my

Beyond the Passage

room, called me every name in the book. I think they were more concerned with the shame than worried about me—or even my immortal soul for that matter. I'd hear them out in this very parlour in the evenings, talking about it. Finally one morning, they told me they were going to send me away. That I was going to have the baby over in New Brunswick and give it away over there so no one would ever know."

She paused. "What could I do? I said yes.

"Father wanted me to go right away before people started to notice but it took a couple of weeks to organize everything. One day I was on my way to the post office to mail that letter to Matthew and I ran into Penny. She was in an awful state, just beside herself and at first I thought something had happened to Matthew. She said no, she'd just come from the doctors. He'd examined her and told her she had a Fallopian tube blockage and would never be able to have children. She was devastated."

I had been concentrating as hard as I could, trying to understand, but this made no sense to me. "But she had my father," I said.

The look she gave me then was a mix of sorrow and regret. "Just hear me out," she said gently.

"I'd never seen Penny like that. She had to deliver the news to Matthew, Matthew who wanted so much to be a father. That's when the idea occurred to me, right then and there. My mind was in a kind of fever. I blurted out the news of my pregnancy. She was taken aback, of course, stunned, as anyone who knew me would be. I explained my plans to put the child up for adoption. It was the only solution. She put her arms around me and held me for a long time.

"She took my arm and we walked up front street towards the church. She was so kind, so gentle with me. Never asked me who the father was. Finally I asked if she might want to adopt my baby. She looked at me and I could tell that the same idea had occurred to her. When she started to speak, I stopped her in mid-sentence. I said I could go to Saint John as planned and she could leave a few weeks later, making sure that everyone knew she was having a baby. We would arrange for her to take the child soon after the

35

Jim Prime

birth at which point she would come home and wait for Matthew's return from the war. She was intrigued but something was holding her back.

"'No one need ever know the baby wasn't yours,' I said. And then added, 'Even Matthew.' She stopped and turned to face me. I can still see the look on her face. 'He'll think the child was,' I said '... from both of you. He knows nothing about your doctor's visit.'"

The effort of recalling these painful memories was taking a toll on Gertrude and I suggested we stop but she insisted that we continue.

"We walked on until we reached the church," she said, "then went in and sat in the back pew. There was no one else around. The church smelled of varnish and flowers and candle wax. I knew that my mother and father looked on it as place of righteous wrath and judgment, a place you went only to escape eternal damnation. I had always thought of it as a sanctuary, a place of community and forgiveness and compassion, and hope. I could see the ray of hope shine in Penny's eyes and then disappear.

"'Matthew will know,' she said. "'He'll know it's not his child.'"

"That's when I told her the whole story. That the child was Matt's. She was struck dumb, attempting to process what I had said. Then she slapped my face very hard. I was glad she did.

"I told her that it was not Matt's fault—that he was only trying to be kind, that he felt sorry for me."

"'You really have no idea, do you?' she shot back.

"'About what?' I said.

"'All the boys were crazy for you. I think Matthew has always loved you.'

"'That's nonsense,' I said. 'He feels so guilty. He loves you. He wants to have children with you. It happened and it's over and I mean nothing to him. He's the best person I know but he loves you.'

"'He doesn't know, then...that you're pregnant?'

"'No,' I said and took the envelope from my pocket. 'I was about to mail this when I saw you.'

"I opened it and handed her the letter. I watched as her eyes

36

scanned the page, silently mouthing the words as she read them. When she had finished, she handed it back to me.

"That's when we both cried, clutching each other as if we were drowning and each was trying to save the other.

"I begged her to think over my offer. Matt need never know but that was up to her, I said. This could be his child, their child. I would have no rights to him, nor would I interfere. I offered to stay in New Brunswick and live there.

"'Who would care for your parents?' she asked me. I ignored the question.

"When she spoke again it was calmly, but with a finality that made any response pointless. 'You will move back a few months after I return with the baby. You'll see the child grow. You and I are the only ones who will ever know.'"

Gertrude stopped abruptly, totally spent, emptied of a cache of secreted memories that she alone had been left heir to. Her face relaxed and she leaned her head back against the chesterfield and closed her eyes.

"Tell your father I would like to see him. Would you do me that kindness, Daniel?"

5

When dad got home from the store later that night, I gave him Gertrude's message. During his lunch break the following day, I watched from our porch as he cut through the school yard and went into her house.

He was in there for a long time and when he came out he went directly back to the store. I followed and waited outside until a customer left and he was alone. When I entered he looked up as if he were expecting me.

Neither of us spoke for a minute and then my father broke the awkward silence. "How do you feel about all this, Daniel?"

I hesitated. "I guess I'm okay," I said. "How about you, Dad?"

He came out from behind the counter and stood in front of me.

Jim Prime

"I'm guess I'm okay too," he said, and gave me a hug.

6

Things changed for us after that. Our acceptance of the situation was only the first step. Soon we welcomed it and, as our relationship with Gertrude grew and deepened, we embraced it wholeheartedly.

Gertrude's relationship with the village also changed, although more subtly. She was seen out and about a little bit more, at the post office or the bank or at church. If the distance wasn't too great, she walked, other times church friends drove her. She made weekly trips by foot to my father's store, where she would give him her grocery list and they would talk as he carefully filled the order. Then he'd place the Back Soon sign in the window, take her by the arm and slowly walk her back home.

Once a month we'd invite Gertrude for Sunday dinner. Afterwards, over coffee, I'd get out the photo albums and she'd scan them carefully for familiar faces. When she found one, there was always a story to go with it. Some were happy, some sad. Whenever she came across a picture of Matthew, her eyes lingered on it for an extra moment before she moved on.

When Will turned 90, the village threw him a party at the IOOF Hall and Gertrude came. They were seated together at a decorated table in the middle of the room and throughout the evening people dropped by to chat and wish them well. Finally there was just the two of them, sitting side by side, eating cake and sharing stories.

~

Thirty years have passed since the summer that Gertrude told us about the bargain she had struck with my grandmother. The grey house at the top of the lane has long since been torn down to make room for a new consolidated school.

Gertrude died at the age of 95 and is buried in a shaded corner of the cemetery, far from the Robbins family plot, but not far from

Beyond the Passage

Penny and Matthew. It was a nice funeral. Because she had no direct family left, my father spoke and afterwards, at the reception, lots of people told him how well he'd done.

Will Thurber lived to the ripe old age of 99 and died while rowing his boat across the cove one still Sunday morning in September. My father and mother are still in good health and I visit them every summer at our house on the lane.

I often think of those summer days back on the island, carefree days that seemed to go on forever. I think of my childhood friends, some who never left and others that I've lost touch with. I think of the village and its people—hard-working and modest and asking little of life. Sometimes, my own memories intertwine with those that were passed along from Gertrude and Will and I try to imagine what life must have been like for them.

As for me, after high school I went away to university where I met and married my wife, Brenda. We have a son, Matt, and two daughters, Penelope and Gertrude. We just call them Penny and Gertie.

Jim Prime

Jessie and Esther

They walked along the side of the gravel road, arms linked, clinging so tightly to each other that their bodies appeared to be fused from shoulders to hips. From a distance the impression was of a single large woman, robust but deformed, her proportions destroyed by a bulky appendage on her left side.

They were mother and daughter, a middle-aged woman and a twenty-something girl. Their arms were entwined, and the head of the smaller woman nestled against the taller one's upper arm. Jessie, the mother, walked aggressively and with purpose, as if on a mission. Esther, the appendage, had little choice but to match her stride. If she slowed her mother's pace at all, it was only slightly; she was borne along like a cork in a rapids. As they drew closer it became clear that the older woman was ruddy faced and robust, the younger pale and fragile.

Twice a week, they left their house and began their two-mile trek into our village. It was an event as predictable as the sun's rising or the noon factory whistle.

They looked straight ahead in the manner of advancing soldiers, oblivious to everything around them. They moved past small clusters of houses and stretches of tree-lined pastures, past the old cemetery on the left and the Department of Highways depot on the right, and continued down Crocker's Hill, past the Freeport United Baptist Church, and into the heart of the community.

Regardless of weather or season, both women wore long, style-resistant cloth coats, frayed at the hems. Handkerchiefs covered their heads, tied tightly under their chins. Their stockings were thick and brown and practical, like bark on a spruce tree. Their shoes were black and blunt, with imperceptible heels.

Beyond the Passage

They were known to everyone as Jessie and Esther and when islanders spoke of them, they ran the names together, as is often the case with twins. We did not use their last names. You never mentioned one without the other, you never saw one without the other.

Defiance was embedded in the mother's face. It was the look of a martyr willing to fight for her beliefs—even anxious to provoke a fight for them. She found vice and wickedness lurking virtually everywhere within the confines of our small fishing village.

Her daughter Esther's face was fish-belly white, gaunt, and sickly. She was timid in the manner of a small dog. But she had no bark, no bravado, false or otherwise. Her features reflected her anxiety, as if she was waiting for some terrible force to strike her down at any moment. She clung to her mother, studiously avoiding eye contact as much as possible. Esther absorbed the world in furtive glances she periodically shot toward those who approached. The outside world was a dangerous and evil place and she braced herself for assaults that awaited her around every turn.

Jessie and Esther were Pentecostals and Jessie was full to overflowing with the Holy Spirit. Often this spirit would overtake her and she would shout "Praise the lord" or "Hallelujah" for no reason apparent to us. At other times she would quote Bible verses that seemed out of context to the occasion.

But there was method to her apparent madness. She was aware that people were watching her as she passed and was prepared to unholster her religious fervour with lightning speed at the slightest provocation.

Like many with this heightened level of passion, she found fault in the most innocent of things. On one occasion, the Pentecostals joined with the Baptists to sponsor a Saturday-night revival meeting under a big tent in a field overlooking Grand Passage. On a whim, my teenage sister Margaret and two of her friends decided to go and dressed up for the occasion. When they entered the canvas church, Jessie swept down on them like an avenging angel, rebuking them for "painting their temples," an accusation that both amused and puzzled them.

Next morning at the breakfast table, Margaret related the story

41

Jim Prime

to our mother, who explained that Jesse had been scolding the girls for wearing lipstick. The temples she referred to were their God-given face and efforts to enhance them were blasphemous.

Her other lasting memory from the event would become an oft-quoted line from the visiting evangelist, an evocative reference to the ability of the Holy Spirit to go "up through the ceiling, and never even crack the plaster."

My own direct experience with Jessie and Esther came when my come-from-away cousins and I were painting my dad's general store one warm August afternoon. From his perch atop a ladder, David, at 14 the oldest of us three, saw the mother and daughter pass by and shouted, "Praise the Lord."

Jessie swung around so quickly that Esther was almost dislodged from her moorings. My younger cousin Lindsay and I cowered as she strode back and stood beneath the ladder and unleashed a fiery diatribe of biblical condemnation worthy of a Mississippi preacher. "You come here from the big city and think you own the place. Your father is a hypocrite. Pretends to be a Christian. And you kids are going straight to hell if you don't mend your ways."

My vacationing uncle, you see, was a theologian of some repute, a professor of theology at the University of Southern California.

At that time, the sixties, anyone who returned with even a modicum of success to his humble origins was suspect. The reflexive reaction was to think that they were lording it over those whom they had left behind. The villagers even had a name for such people—whitewashed Yankees.

That was decidedly not the case with my uncle, who treasured his island heritage and drove 4000 miles every summer to this summer paradise. But he had the dreaded Dr. in front of his name and he drove a brand new Buick LeSabre, and occasionally he even smoked a "rum flavoured and wine dipped" cigarillo—these facts branded him as wealthy and possibly debauched.

Jessie's Christianity was inextricably linked to simple and fundamental truths. My uncle's religion was too philosophical, too welcoming, too non-judgmental for her. She railed at my poor

42

Beyond the Passage

cousin for a full five minutes, began a huffy retreat and then swung back around to land further verbal blows for another five because she had forgotten to point out that his sermons were lacking in hellfire and damnation. When she finally stomped away, we were spent, until a wisecrack from my older cousin, albeit stated in subdued tones, restored us.

Not that Jessie didn't have reason to be angry. It was an ill-advised comment from my cousin and this had not been an isolated incident. Many young boys and teenagers knew that they could get a rise out of her with a simple Hallelujah or some other mocking comment.

At such times I felt sorry for Esther, who had said nothing but was subjected to scorn by association, passive scorn that she was ill-equipped to counter. She was so pale, so vulnerable, so lacking in anything that faintly resembled joy, let alone the joy of God. The world must have been a frightening place for this pasty, unsubstantial young woman. I couldn't help but wonder if she had ever been invited to a party, ever had friends; if she even knew how to carry on a conversation outside the presence of her mother. In fact I wondered if she was ever outside this domineering presence.

From what we could see, her mother wasn't intentionally unkind to her—quite the opposite. She treated her as if she were a helpless bird who needed constant care and protection. She provided the cage and this bird would never wander far, its wings having been clipped and re-clipped repeatedly over her 20-odd years.

Esther was given to occasional seizures, or fits. There was some disagreement over whether these fits were manifestations of the spirit moving within her or the devil attempting to take control—or a struggle between the two. A medical explanation ran third or fourth in the minds of her fellow congregants.

Of course it's more than likely that the condition could have been controlled, even alleviated today. Whether the cause was physical or metaphysical, there is little doubt that the fits were triggered by the picture of the world her mother had planted in her head and carefully cultivated throughout her life. It was the

Jim Prime

worst possible combination—an excitable, driven mother and a submissive, damaged daughter.

My sympathy for Esther grew whenever I saw her. She was like a prisoner. We had read *To Kill a Mockingbird* in school that year and I couldn't help but think that she would have made a perfect companion, or at least suitable suitor, for Boo Radley. Perhaps, I thought, the two lost souls would find something in each other that they had never had before—acceptance perhaps, or some common philosophy.

Perhaps they would start slowly until trust was established and then ever so gradually begin to talk with each other. Small things at first. Keeping each other company in a lonely and dangerous world. And then one day they would share ideas, their likes and dislikes. They would wander outside and sit on the porch on a fine summer evening and drink something cool and refreshing.

A metamorphosis would follow, slow and steady. They would never mix with many people. They would keep to themselves. But they would no longer fear the world so much. They would be as free as those with clipped wings could ever be free.

A few years later I saw an obituary for Jessie in the *Chronicle-Herald*. It offered little information. She had died of a heart attack while walking through the village with her daughter. The obituary ended with a Bible passage, but I can't recall what it was.

My thoughts immediately moved to Esther. What would happen to Esther? What happens to a living appendage when the host is gone?

The party game

Last Saturday night my wife and I went to a Valentine's party. Joanie and Hugh Sheppard, a couple we had recently met through a mutual friend, had invited us. Truth be told, I didn't really want to go. It'd been a long week and the Leafs were playing the Canadiens that night on *Hockey Night in Canada*.

But the Sheppards seemed like very nice people and really wanted us to come. Joanie told us that she had put a lot of thought into selecting interesting but diverse couples whom she felt would hit it off. So we decided to go. It *was* Valentine's Day after all.

We don't go out socially all that much and so were unfashionably punctual, but the other invitees arrived within minutes and introductions were made. There were six couples in all, including our hosts. None of us knew the others, although I recognized a couple of people that I'd seen around town.

We went into the well-appointed living room and, under the seemingly effortless direction of the host, gave our drink preferences and received the results. Halting conversations began as people struggled to find points of connection.

At this awkward juncture, our hostess announced that in order to get to know each other and 'break the ice', we would divide into pairs and spend 15 minutes gathering information from our assigned partner. We were then to return to the living room and, one after the other, each person was to divulge five interesting facts about his or her subject.

I don't much like party games, but at least this one had a purpose and so I was determined to enter into the spirit of the whole thing. We recharged our glasses, and the six twosomes dispersed to corners of the living room, the kitchen, the dining room, and the

Jim Prime

guest bedroom which was just off the kitchen.

My partner and I ended up at the kitchen table. He turned out to be a 62-year-old man named Ian, with a slight build, a gentle demeanour, and a monotone voice. I agreed he should interview me first, and he methodically extracted some facts about my life as an author, my love of baseball and the names and current statuses of our two children and two grandchildren. When he was confident that he had memorized at least five items, and a couple of spares just in case, it was my Wolf Blitzer moment.

I quickly found out that Ian was on his second marriage, that he had worked all his life in banks, first in England and then in various RBC branches across Nova Scotia. It was, frankly, pretty boring stuff, and I knew that other couples would not know him any better than I now did after I related these dry facts.

So, on a whim, I asked Ian to tell me the most outrageous thing he'd ever done, hoping that perhaps this mild little man had skydived or bungee jumped, or something.

He paused and gazed toward the ceiling as he tried to think of something. "Well," he finally said, "once I was driving along the Bedford Highway on my way to work in Halifax. I had left home a bit late and, for once, there wasn't much inbound traffic. All of a sudden a car appeared behind me and rode my bumper for a solid kilometre until there was a gap in the oncoming traffic. Then he laid on his horn and passed me, giving me the finger as he went by. Very dangerous.

"I decided to follow him and get his plate number so that I could report him and maybe save someone's life. The man was clearly a menace.

"We passed Mt. St. Vincent University on the right and the container pier on the left, and when we got to the traffic lights at the corner of Lady Hammond Road and Windsor Street, he turned left and headed toward the new bridge. Funny, I still call it the new bridge even though it's been there, what, fifty years? The A. Murray MacKay Bridge to give it its proper name."

He shook his head ruefully. "There were several vehicles between us as we drove onto the span but I kept an eye on him as

Beyond the Passage

best I could. By the time we reached the toll booth on the Dartmouth side, I was only three cars behind and I followed him as he continued on along Route 111 toward the Mic Mac interchange. He exited onto Burnside Drive and entered the Burnside Industrial Park. He went a couple of blocks, took a left and then a right onto Ilsley Avenue. At this point, I was directly behind him but he didn't see me. My car meant nothing to him."

Ian paused to take a drink of red wine, smacking his lips in obvious approval of the vintage. I could feel my attention wandering, and stifled a yawn.

"So anyway," he continued, "he continues up Ilsley and pulls into this little strip mall affair and drives around back and parks his Audi. Did I mention that he was driving an Audi? A silver-coloured Audi. Nice-looking vehicle. Anyway, he parks behind a business called Executive Lighting, one of those high end shops for yuppies. He gets out of his car and that's when he notices me for the first time, although he still doesn't recognize me. I get out of my Honda Civic and approach him. He's a tall man, 6'4, 6'5 maybe, but not an ounce of fat on him. He obviously works out. I say, 'Hey you cut me off back there on the Bedford Highway. You could have killed someone. Please have a little respect for other drivers next time. I could have had a child aboard.' I'm polite but forceful, you know?

"Well, you'd have thought I spit in his face. His face got red and he moved toward me. Boy, the language that came out of that man's mouth. Pure filth. It was pretty obvious that he was going to hit me, so I kept moving away until my back was against the wall of the business. He smiled—more of a leer really—and said some more nasty things that I won't repeat. I noticed a rusty iron bar on the ground. It had been a spindle in the railing that led up the three concrete steps to the rear entrance. Well, I grabbed that thing and I held it up, just to warn him off, you know? But he kept coming until he was just a couple of feet away. I closed my eyes and swung. The impact made a sickening sound—sort of like when you crack a walnut—and when I opened my eyes it was like his head had exploded or something. He fell like a rock and a huge pool of blood immediately formed around him. I didn't check for a pulse. It was

Jim Prime

obvious that he was dead. I dropped the rod, got back in my car and drove away."

At that point the hostess poked her head around the corner and said, "Time's up, boys. Can't wait to hear all your little secrets."

Betrayal

I woke from a fitful sleep to see narrow shafts of sunlight filtering through the grove of white birches across the clearing. Sometime overnight the hard rain had finally ended and outside my cramped enclosure the world was sodden and green and glistening. Tree tops swayed in the still-swirling wind, shaking off water like dogs emerging from a swim. The small recess at the bottom of a 12-foot rock face had provided me a measure of shelter from the downpour but could not prevent the dampness from invading my body.

Every part of me was aching from the hard surface. As I stretched and struggled to stand up, coming to life in segments like a blow-up mattress, a fierce chill gripped me. I pulled the flask of Jack Daniels from the inside pocket of my jacket and took a long draft. I was rewarded with a rush of warmth that spread rapidly through my body and dissolved the cobwebs from my mind.

I was now fully awake and suddenly famished. I rifled through my backpack for the ration kit and grabbed two protein bars, devouring the first one quickly and savouring the second.

I knew that skilled trackers would be among the pursuers, most likely some I had helped train. They would be scouring the woods and, now that the rain had ceased, it would only be a matter of time before the dogs picked up the scent.

Even as I was forming that thought, the muffled baying of bloodhounds arrived on the wind. I had heard them periodically the previous day, only to have the sounds fade and disappear, but now the howls were insistent, focused, and louder.

I took another swig from the flask before returning it to my pocket. Then I shouldered my backpack and rifle and set out in the direction of the emerging sun. I left the open clearing and was

Jim Prime

swallowed up in the relative darkness of the forest, the dancing, jagged shadows of spruce and fir trees playing tricks on my eyes.

Within a half hour the sun had risen far enough to offer more light and my pace increased. I pushed my way through a large thicket of alders, receiving repeated slaps across my face and cold water down my neck, and emerged onto what appeared to be an abandoned logging trail, overgrown from disuse but a path forward, nonetheless.

The waterlogged earth made each step laborious, and I comforted myself with the knowledge that hunters and prey faced the same challenges. In truth, the trail was not unlike the obstacle courses that every enlisted man was forced to overcome. Fallen trees, and gullies left behind by the spring run-off, tested my mettle. The rough terrain required my full attention and it took a while to realize that I'd been climbing steadily. My boots slipped on the mossy rocks beneath my feet. I took note of the uprooted trees and natural rock crevices that offered adequate hiding places if I needed one.

Another hour passed before the ground levelled to a plateau where the logging path abruptly ended. I paused, hands on knees, to recover my breath and my resolve. The wind had completely died out and the only sound was the intermittent baying of the dogs. I estimated they must be less than a half mile behind me. I took a deep breath and trudged onward.

I moved with stealth, stopping every so often to listen before advancing. During one of these pauses, I thought I heard something, a snapping twig perhaps, or the rustle of fallen leaves. My heart jumped and my pulse quickened as I stood still and waited. A pair of squirrels scampered past me and bounded single file up an ancient oak tree. My sudden panic embarrassed me and I uttered a quiet curse.

Within minutes I found myself on the edge of a small opening in the trees. The faint, acrid smell of doused firewood reached my nostrils.

I retreated beyond the tree line and began to walk along the perimeter of the clearing. I was acutely aware of every step I took,

Beyond the Passage

my senses keen, awakened to the probability that I was being watched. My army training had prepared me for moments like this and yet my hands shook.

My fears were confirmed when I felt the unmistakable, unyielding hardness of a rifle barrel pressed against my back. I froze in place, fighting a foolhardy impulse to reach for my rifle.

"Make one move," I heard him say, "and I'll separate your head from your shoulders. Understand?"

I nodded, my back still to the gunman.

"Turn around slowly," he said.

I did turn slowly, my hands involuntarily rising in surrender. Private Prentice's face was distorted by fear and desperation but it was definitely him.

"Son of a bitch," he said, taking a step back and lowering his gun, if only slightly. "Sergeant Walters, I sure as hell didn't expect you."

"Count yourself lucky, private," I managed to say. "The guys back there aren't nearly as forgiving."

He looked at me for a long moment and then dropped his gun onto the mossy ground in front of him. He dropped to his knees, cupped his head in both hands and began to sob, his body shaking uncontrollably.

I waited for the wave of emotion to subside. When he had regained a measure of control, I helped him to his feet, put my hands on his shoulders and looked him directly in the eyes. "Private, if you want to live, you have to be honest with me. If you are, I'll do my best to protect you."

He nodded. His face was smeared with camouflage paint, dirt, dried blood, and, now, tears.

"Okay. I need to know how much money you cheated those men out of."

He bristled. "I have never cheated at cards in my life," he said firmly.

"I know you were part of a gambling ring at camp. I also know that sometimes those poker games got out of hand and some men lost their entire pay packets. The officers caught on and were about to close it down when this happened. I assume that you

Jim Prime

were the big winner, because I overheard the men talking at the mess. One guy said he was going to shoot you on sight. Why would they want to kill you, private? Unless you cheated them. What happened to get us out here in the middle of nowhere with armed men closing in?"

"What the hell?" he said. "I'm already facing court-marshal. My family will be devastated. My fiancé will never speak to me again."

"So you did cheat? Listen, Prentice, we take it to the lieutenant. You'll get a few demerits, you'll have to pay the men back, maybe even get some punishment, but it isn't the end of the world."

"No! No, I told you I did not cheat! I'm not bluffing. In fact I lost more money than anyone."

I was genuinely confused. "Then what? What is this all about? Do you owe them money? Is that it?"

He began to turn away, but I shook him hard and when he looked back there was a resigned expression on his face.

"I've been a gambler all my life, Sarge. My father says it's a character weakness, that I have an addictive personality." He snorted derisively. "That's why he forced me to join up. So I wouldn't besmirch the family name. He was a career man—General Philip P. Prentice, pretty big man in military circles, as you know. 'It'll make or break you,' he said. 'Get you away from all those temptations. No time for gambling in the army,' he said. Boy, was dear old dad ever wrong about that."

"Okay, okay. But there has to be more to it than losing at cards. The men in the mess hall were like a lynch mob. They wanted to kill you. I was trying to calm them down when someone came in and said they'd seen you going into the woods at the southeast edge of the base. They all rushed out like they were after Osama himself. I tried to stop them but they had blood in their eyes. You're lucky they miscalculated. They figured you were making your way up to the highway."

I listened for a moment for the pursuers. "I guess I'm a bit of a gambler, too. I took a chance that you struck out cross country, toward the border. And I was right. By the time the rest caught on, I was hot on your trail. But while you and I holed up last night, their hatred drove them on through the rain. They're right on your heels. You've heard them. If I'm going to help, you have to tell me exactly why they're after you."

He looked at me for a long moment before replying. "You could call it a high stakes gamble." His face was now composed, hard to read. "In fact the highest. There have to be winners and losers in gambling. You understand that, don't you Sarge? Any military man knows that before they sign those enlistment papers. You could end up at this forgotten little base on the Mexican border where the only 'enemy' is some poor family looking for a better life...or you could end up in some shithole like Afghanistan, facing ISIS."

There was a long pause. The private seemed to be assessing the hand he'd been dealt. "I guess you have to know when to fold 'em," he said with a shrug. "I've done a terrible thing, Sarge." He spoke as if in a trance.

"What? What did you do?"

"I killed those four men."

"What are you talking about?"

"The men who were killed on exercises last month. I killed them."

I was stunned. "But that was an accident. Somehow live ammo got mixed in with the blanks...The review panel investigated. Their conclusion was human error by persons unknown. They said a fuck-up at the depot was most likely responsible. They said—"

"It was no accident," he said. "I mixed the live ammo in with the blanks."

I stood there, mouth open. No words came to me. In the near distance I heard isolated shouts as the dogs and men crashed through the underbrush.

"But why?" I stammered. "Why would you do such a thing? These are your brothers, your comrades. Why would you want them dead?"

He hesitated before answering. "It was nothing personal, Sarge. Just a sporting proposition."

He saw the look of disbelief on my face. "There were four guys in the unit who were into me for over eight thousand dollars. They

Jim Prime

said they'd call my father if I didn't pay up. I knew I couldn't stall them much longer. I figured there had to be a way out. It wasn't hard to steal the keys to the ordinance supply room. I mixed the live ammo with the blanks and went back to the barracks and went to bed. I didn't sleep much, though."

"You mean to tell me that you—?"

"Yes Sarge. It was no sure thing, though. Not like betting on a prize fight that's been fixed. There's no sport in that. I pay my debts and I would have paid these, too, if it hadn't worked out the way it did. I just raised the ante, is all. There's about 200 rounds in a box of blanks. I mixed in 100 rounds of live ammo. The odds were 2-1 against me. I don't know anyone in Vegas who wouldn't jump on a wager like that.

"There were four of them—Mattson, O'Leary, Smith and Ziegler. When they divided us into two platoons for the war games, Ziegler ended up on my side the other three in the enemy group. That meant I could shoot at three of them myself—but my ammo was mixed, too. Like I say, I don't cheat. It wasn't as easy as I thought. I have to admit that my training really did kick in. I worked hard to get those three guys and I succeeded.

"And it wasn't as if I wasn't in real danger. I mean, this was double or nothing for me. Any of those shots could have killed me. And then Mattson stood up from behind the barrier and just like that, one of our snipers shot him dead. I knew then it was my lucky day. Of course no one knew they were actually dead until later, when the lieutenant blew his whistle and the firing stopped. Even then, it took a while…lots of confusion and panic…"

The haunted look of fear and regret that had been in his eyes had now been replaced by excitement and thrill. He was actually grinning. "I had a clear shot at O'Leary and I think I flat out missed. Could have been a dud, but in fairness, I think I rushed the shot. I kept watching his position and, sure enough, he stuck his head up again. I fired two quick rounds. The second one was no dud. I struck him on the left temple and he slumped forward. That left Smith. I scanned the trees with my field glass but couldn't spot him. That's when I knew that lady luck was with me again. He

Beyond the Passage

charged across the field toward us, holding a grenade. Mr. Big Man. I raised my rifle to fire, but before I could, Johnson, just to the left of me, pulled the trigger and dropped him. He fell like a sack of wet cement. To me it was obvious he was dead. To the rest, it was just part of the exercise." His eyes sparkled.

"But then I did something I'm ashamed of."

"What do you mean?"

"I cheated."

"Cheated?"

"Ziegler was a good soldier, one of those career guys who actually wanted to see action. He was too savvy to get shot and he'd scored several hits on the other side. I had a few rounds of live ammo in my pocket. I knew the lieutenant was about to blow the whistle to end the exercise. I loaded a live round and ducked down, out of sight of the rest. Ziegler was about twenty yards behind me. I aimed and hit him in the heart."

There was a pause when the enormity of what he'd done seemed to sink in. "I'm not proud of that," he said. "Like dealing from a marked deck."

And then the grin returned to his face. "There were other casualties, of course, but the only fatalities were my four poker buddies. Luckiest day of my life."

The dogs were getting closer and I could hear the men cursing and grunting. The private turned toward the sound. When he turned back my rifle was levelled at his head.

"You're a gambling man, Private," I said. "I got my ammo from that same supply. Maybe the odds are still with you."

I pulled the trigger. The sharp crack pierced the still air and echoed repeatedly off the surrounding trees, like volleys from a firing squad.

I sat down on the soft moss to wait for my comrades. "You lose, private." I said, reaching for the last of the Jack Daniels.

Jim Prime

The party line

I carefully lifted the phone from its cradle and was relieved that the conversation continued, with no indication either party knew I was listening. The first few seconds were key, because if they didn't notice right away, they probably wouldn't notice at all.

It was just one of thousands of calls I'd intercepted over the years but this one would change everything.

It's really an art form. In some ways—only some, mind you, it's akin to being a secret agent, a spy. You need nerves of steel and a tight-lipped reticence that few can master.

Obviously you have to be patient and do some pre-planning, like making sure there's no radio playing in the background. Pets are the worst. They're too unpredictable. A single dog's bark could prove fatal.

Some people were just dumb about it, holding the phone too close to the parakeet cage, or even stroking a cat. Meows are loud and, believe it or not, even purrs can be audible. Never cook supper while listening and never—never, ever—eat.

Being caught can result in embarrassment all around. People frown upon third-party monitors like myself. Like deer-jacking and weekday drinking, it just isn't done. Except that it is, all the time.

I had already dealt with the moral issue, whether it was ethical to listen in on other people's private conversations. After considerable thought and some prayer, I had decided that it was harmless, victimless, like insurance fraud.

My mother, who sits in her wheelchair by the wood stove most of the day, disagrees, of course, but she's from a different generation and doesn't understand that these are the sixties, when anything goes. She gets very agitated when the phone rings and I pick

Beyond the Passage

it up. She looks at me disapprovingly and shakes her finger at me. She can barely speak, but sometimes she motions me closer to her and tells me that I wasn't raised that way, that it was wrong.

I disagree. After all, who am I hurting? Life can get tedious for a bachelor living with his agèd mother. It was just a diversion, like watching TV. Livening up a long winter evening by listening to some gossip is hardly one of the seven deadly sins. It's really no different than overhearing a conversation at the post office or the coffee shop. It even helps to build a sense of community in my opinion. I really believe that.

Or at least I did until a recent incident.

I was fortunate. My number was 74 ring 2, meaning that if the phone sounded two short rings, it was for me. If it was one ring, or one long and one short or three short or two short and one long, it was for someone else. Each household had their own custom ring. I now knew them all: who had the best calls, and who was scarcely worth listening in on.

Of course, the prize number on my circuit was the doctor's office. Good old 74, ring one. One short, sharp jingle.

And it was mine. All mine. The beauty of having the doctor on my line was that emergency calls sometimes came in late at night when mother was sleeping. I could give my full attention to the conversation without her sad eyes and worried expression distracting me.

There were other numbers that I frequented. I knew that two longs was Mrs. Barnaby from across the cove, and that if it was Friday night, it was her daughter calling from Toronto to catch up on events of the week.

Very interesting young woman, Mrs. Barnaby's daughter. I knew her when she was just a school girl. Later, she got a job as a window dresser at Eaton's on Yonge Street and led a very exciting life. One day she had seen Pierre Berton walk right past her into the store. Another time, Bruno Gerussi and his wife had stopped in front of a window she was dressing and he had smiled and nodded to her.

Of course, I had this news before anyone else in the village—

Jim Prime

which could be tricky, because when I visited the general store and someone told the story about Mrs. Barnaby's daughter, having heard it from Mrs. Barnaby directly, I felt cheated somehow. After all, aside from Mrs. Barnaby herself, I was the first on the islands to know. I was forced to smile and feign mild surprise when I wanted to be able to say, "I already knew that!"

Very frustrating! What was the good of discovering all this news if you couldn't use it?

I didn't dare tell mother, of course. Finally I decided that the joy was in the discovery itself. Once I made peace with that, I received enormous inner satisfaction and even enjoyed hearing others talk about things I had learned hours and even days earlier.

I'm sure some people observed the knowing, enigmatic smile on my face. No doubt it gave me an air of mystery and, dare I say, a nonchalance that was alluring to the opposite sex.

I also got satisfaction in comparing the accuracy of their third-hand accounts with the first-hand, straight-from-the-horse's-mouth version I had so diligently obtained from the source, complete with the inflections and spontaneous emotion that were lost in the stale retellings during brief encounters at the post office or in line at the bank.

Some people might say this was gloating, but since I didn't actually *say anything*, that charge can hardly be justified. In fact, I'd venture to say that, since I kept a precise record of each conversation in my diary, my version of events might be more accurate than that of those who were engaged in said conversation. How ironic is that?

I like to think that I even captured the spirit as well as the exact content of each call, using exclamation marks and ellipses where appropriate. I can never thank my grade nine teacher, Mrs. Hooper, enough for drumming these grammatical conventions into my resisting brain.

One of my biggest fears has always been that I might get caught up in a conversation and inadvertently join in. I'd come close more than once. When I heard that little Joanie Israel had been playing in a punt and the punt had drifted away from the wharf and was

Beyond the Passage

being carried out into the Passage, I almost said, "Call the Coast Guard."

I caught myself, thank the good Lord, and little Joanie was fine because someone had already made the call, but it was close. I mean, it's natural, isn't it, to want to join in on conversations, to console or praise or enlighten or laugh? It's only human. We are a social species.

So, as you can see, my hobby is certainly not lacking in excitement and drama.

In the wee hours of Sunday, August 5th, 1965 I had heard Orin Purcell's familiar ring at precisely 12:09 a.m. Even before picking up, I knew it had to be bad news, and knowing something of the drinking habits of Orin's son Paul, I held my breath as the doctor answered. Sure enough, it was Maud, the operator at Central, calling to tell Orin that there had been an accident and he should have his neighbour Johnny Welsh come and stay with him until the RCMP arrived at his house. Orin had seemed stunned and yet resigned, as if he had been expecting it but it had come too soon.

Over the next few days and weeks, I monitored all phone calls to the Purcell line—the RCMP calls, the calls from Paul's sister in Halifax, the Baptist minister calling about funeral arrangements. It kept me quite busy. Like binge-watching a serial on TV, except I was listening, not watching—binge-listening.

Mother's health was failing at that point and she no longer had the energy to object to my hobby.

Anyway, back to the call that changed everything. One early December evening, I was just finishing the dishes and heard the phone ring—one sharp but somehow insistent note. It was the doctor's ring. So I went into the living room, sat in the recliner and very carefully picked up the receiver, smooth as silk. Perfect. The hardest part was over.

I lit a cigarette, careful to cover the mouthpiece when I flicked the lighter.

A woman was already in mid-sentence, clearly agitated, but struggling to control it. "I don't care anymore. I have to see you now. Johnny's out fishing and I'm here all alone. I'll meet you at the

Jim Prime

camp. No one will see us there."

The doc put up a small argument, but then caved in and said he'd be there in one hour.

Well, I knew who the woman was. Very pretty. Very sexy. And I knew where their cottage was, too, halfway up the island, with lots of trees around it and a big window to give them a view of the lake.

I made a snap decision, got dressed and jumped in my car. I parked on a little logging road out of sight and walked down to the cottage. It was less than a mile off the road. I squatted there and waited.

The doctor was always punctual—I guess they have to be, don't they?—and, sure enough, he arrived right on time. He knocked once and went right in.

They moved out of view for a minute and I figured I was out of luck, but then a light went on in the loft. The large window was wide open and I could hear them talking. There was a tall pine nearby and I knew that it would allow me an excellent view.

I climbed it quietly—stealthily, if I do say so myself—and made myself comfortable on a sturdy limb, leaning against the trunk. I could see everything, like I was at a drive-in movie. And I was hoping the main feature would be X-Rated.

Suddenly I heard twigs snapping and feet clomping. Before I knew it, my tree was surrounded by at least 15 people—and I recognized them all. Some were next-door neighbours. Every person on my party line was there.

The doctor and Phyllis—that was her name—came out and joined them. I was surprised to see that they were fully clothed. It had been a set-up. A sting operation.

In due course I had to appear before a judge in the Digby courthouse, where I received a stern warning—rude, if you ask me—and a small fine. It was embarrassing, but at least my name didn't appear in the newspaper. I guess the *Digby Courier* considered it too trivial to report.

When I finally got home to the islands after that long day, I heated up some day-old chowder and collapsed into my armchair, glad that it was over. The phone was at my side but I studiously avoided even looking at it. I finished my chowder and leafed through a *Reader's Digest* that I'd already read, before tossing it aside.

Once again my eyes were drawn to the phone and, as I was staring at it, it rang, startling me. Two longs—that was Ethel Thomas.

I carefully picked up the receiver. The first thing I heard was my name. Ethel and her sister Ellen were calling me a creep and a pervert and every name in the book. I carefully hung up.

Twenty minutes later, the phone rang again. One long, one short—that was Judson Pyne. I picked up and Judd and Ernie Sullivan were calling me down to the lowest.

I suddenly had a tight knot in the pit of my stomach.

This went on for hours, everyone on my line was saying terrible things about me. Gossiping. Spreading rumours and outright slander—even threats of bodily harm! One woman even said, "I'll bet he's listening to us talk right now." Can you imagine the level of cynicism? It's enough to make you lose all faith in people, it really is.

Still, I couldn't resist picking up the phone every time it rang.

My mother died about a month after the incident. Those who came to the funeral left immediately after, even though I provided a nice variety of finger foods that I bought at Sobey's in Digby.

I'm an old man now and I don't really go out very often, except for weekly trips to the general store, and even then I go early in the morning and come directly back, to avoid people.

As for the phone, I seldom use it any more, even though they replaced the party-line system decades ago.

Small-town people can be so petty and unforgiving. I've decided to move on.

I've purchased a second-hand computer from one of the few people who still talk to me. It's all new to me. I've signed up for Facebook and Instagram and Twitter and a whole bunch of what they call apps.

I confess that I'm enjoying it. People tell you everything about themselves. They even post pictures of themselves and what they're eating. Can you imagine? It's so, oh, I don't know, demo-

Jim Prime

cratic, so open.

I feel rejuvenated and in some ways vindicated. I already have friends in four provinces and six states. And, believe it or not, I'm corresponding with a prince in Saudi Arabia who has presented me with a very attractive financial proposition!

Life is good.

The nudist colony

It was 1967. Three years earlier, the British had invaded North America and the continent surrendered after the Beatles fired just two melodic volleys on The Ed Sullivan Show. Long hair was suddenly in style and pot smoking was becoming a rite of passage, as was something called free love. Various groups were protesting various things, some frivolous, some deadly serious; some pressed their case with chants and signs, some with guns and fists. Bras and draft cards were burning in public squares and the establishment was on edge. It seemed that every university was conducting a study—of the changing role of women, of changing racial attitudes, of changing sexual mores. Popular songs were suddenly laden with sexual innuendo and double entendres. Change was in the air and on the air.

Freeport, a small fishing village clinging to the western shore of Long Island in southwestern Nova Scotia, remained mostly immune to radical change, or at least socially distanced from it. However, crystal-clear radio reception made the Beatles and other airborne infestations the exception. Wistful folk music gave way to hard-edged protest songs about war, racism and women's rights.

There were no actual protests on the island, and if hair was a bit longer than usual it was only because the barber had retired and moved to Digby. The only civil unrest came in the form of fights between Westporters and Freeporters outside Lloyd's dance hall on Saturday nights. These were fuelled not by cannabis or causes, but by Captain Morgan Dark rum, often with a chaser of Ten Penny Old Stock Ale.

In contrast to its people, who cling to tradition, Nova Scotia summers are unpredictable changelings, none more so than those

Jim Prime

we experienced at the mouth of the Bay of Fundy. By definition, islands have very well defined borders and can be as confining and depressing as a prison or as secure and hopeful as a womb depending on many factors, not least of which are the weather and one's state of mind. The former often dictates the latter.

Some days break so clear that you can look out to sea so far that you'd swear that you can discern the outline of Gibraltar. At such times the possibilities, like the horizon, seem endless. Other days are claustrophobic, with oppressive fog banks shrinking the geography and limiting the possibilities.

On this particular Sunday afternoon in mid-August the sun shone down from a blue and cloudless sky. The islands were enjoying a brief respite from the murk that had laid siege in June and enshrouded the shores for most of the summer. Eighty-nine-year old Austin Delaney sat on a hogshead halfway down the government wharf, repairing a herring net.

The noon whistle had just sounded and a group of factory workers emerged from the dank interior of Connor Brothers Ltd., hoping to soak up as much sun as possible during the one-hour break. Their skin was so fish-belly white that they resembled an army of zombies, the sickly pallor making them appear almost translucent to surface dwellers such as myself. They stood together in small groups or perched on overturned trawl tubs near Austin.

Some reached into their pockets for makings and papers and expertly rolled perfectly cylindrical cigarettes. Others carefully removed waxed paper from their sandwiches and unscrewed thermoses of coffee. They spent their working lives in a perpetually-dank environment, carrying out a Dante-esque series of hellish tasks.

Under dim lights, middle-aged men in Barvell aprons gutted fish before others removed their heads and skins. Off to the side, men worked in the gurry bin, shovelling the fish heads, skins, and bones into a rusty trough where a grinding screw rotated upwards from the factory floor and carried the offal through a 4' X 4' aperture in the wall. Outside, seagulls cackled greedily. Outside, seagulls cackled greedily and circled the waiting gurry bin as the feast ar-

Beyond the Passage

rived like take-out orders through the window of a fast-food drive-through.

Austin addressed the newcomers without looking up. "Don't get used to the sunshine, boys," he said. "She's nothing but a weather breeder. Storm's a-comin'."

The men ignored him, squinting at the sun as they quietly smoked and chewed. Not even an old cynic like Delaney could ruin this day.

Austin was the oldest inhabitant in the community. He was completely deaf in one ear and stubbornly refused to use a hearing aid in the other. He was grisled the way only a fisherman can be. Farmers also get wrinkles from long exposure to the sun, but fishermen get it twice, once directly from the sky and once reflected upward from the salt water. After years of this abuse, the skin takes on the appearance and consistency of a piece of rawhide.

When Austin first went out on the water, schooners still passed regularly through the Passage and fish were so plentiful that only certain species were harvested and the rest were thrown back. It was widely thought that Austin had once been a rum runner and had made a small fortune during the days of American prohibition. He never commented directly on these rumours and his habit of quoting scripture for every occasion and circumstance was usually effective in making people lose interest and change the subject.

Despite Austin's forecast, a briny onshore breeze infused the countryside with hope and peace.

It's a fact that country people do not walk for walking's sake. At least not in Digby County in the early sixties. People who did so were highly suspect. There had to be a purpose, otherwise such behaviour was considered frivolous or shady or both. Unless you were on an errand or visiting a neighbour, it probably meant you were up to no good, or a bit strange. Walking for no reason was wandering aimlessly.

On this day, after so much fog, people found reasons to flout this convention—an unnecessary trip to the post office perhaps, or a walk along the beach to collect driftwood for the woodstove.

It was one of those days that made people forget the thirty dis-

Jim Prime

mal ones that that had preceded it. The sun acted as a powerful dose of vitamin D, a much needed anti-depressant. People chatted amiably; neighbours exchanged greetings and life was good.

And then change came to the island with no advance notice. No "red sky in morning, sailors take warning," or "wind from the east, t'ain't good for man nor beast." No radio advisory for Yarmouth to Block Island to alert an unsuspecting citizenry. It just arrived, unannounced and unsummoned, a summer storm that threatened to lay waste to our very way of life. Once it made landfall at the western tip of Long Island, the word spread like contagion. The young factory workers on the wharf had gotten wind of it and were exhibiting unmistakable symptoms of spring fever.

There was a nudist colony on the island.

If it had been a leper colony, the citizenry would have been no more or less aghast. The news had been brought to Curt's general store by Mildred Bates, who had heard it from Carl Doty who had picked it up from Esrum Haines. After that the provenance was somewhat diluted but Esrum, although admittedly part of the aforesaid Captain Morgan's crew, swore he had seen things.

The reports divided the village into various camps with distinct thoughts on the matter. The church people and the IOOF Hall folks saw it as the leading edge of ruination. The fishermen and factory workers, hopeless gossips, wallowed in the news, embellished it, and passed off-colour comments. Finally, there were the teenage boys, of whom I was one. We were curious—extremely, excruciatingly, desperately curious to learn more.

"I heard they was orgies goin' on," said Dave Tibert, a fifteen year old with an almost imperceptible blond moustache and matching chin hair.

"Like fun," Luke Morell said. "Orgies take more than four, and that's all that come."

"Orgies can happen with four, I'm pretty sure," Dale said indignantly. "Anyways, the point is, they walk around buck naked."

A lack of facts creates a vacuum which nature and human nature despise and rush to fill.

Details were scarce, but it seems there indeed had been sight-

Beyond the Passage

ings of excessive skin and body parts over at the old farm, just beyond the gravel pit, overlooking St. Mary's Bay. It was a secluded spot accessible only by an old dirt road from which large, deeply embedded rocks protruded. The farm had been vacant for many years after the death, without a will, of Charlie Youngerer.

Finally a nephew living in Halifax was able to establish a claim to the property. He wasn't interested in moving to the remote outpost and immediately put it up for sale or lease, advertising it in Boston as a place to get away from it all, back to nature, where you can still hear yourself think.

Sure enough, within a month the realtor's sign at the entrance to the farm road had been removed. The place had been leased.

This news was shocking to villagers who saw no value in this land, or any land if it came to that. They questioned who would want a rickety old farmhouse and a rocky, fit-for-nothing farm out in the woods? "Must be crazy, on the dope," was the popular refrain.

Within weeks a moving van was seen turning onto the road and slowly grinding its way toward the farm. In actual fact, news of the arrival had preceded the van to Freeport. The CB radio crowd had long since established an early warning system to inform one another when "the Mounties are down" from Digby. The heads-up allowed time for miscreants to cease any illegal activity for a few hours: deer jacking, bootlegging, drinking and driving, speeding, and general disturbing of the peace.

The lookout at the Tiverton wharf, ten miles to the east, relayed word to all and sundry as the Thompson's Transfer truck drove up the slip, followed by a late model Volkswagen minivan obviously containing the new owners. The initial report suggested there were three girls and three boys, all in their late teens or early twenties—enough for an orgy by anyone's standard.

For a while all was quiet. There were a few random sightings as the young people ventured into the village to buy milk and bread and other staples but little else to satisfy public curiosity.

Of course people wondered what they were up to. Did they have any connection to the island? Were they those hippies like the ones

Jim Prime

who had nested in Bear River?

The mystery deepened and speculation was rampant. And then came the revelation that struck like a savage norEaster. Two fishermen were returning from hand-lining cod just beyond Gull Rock. As they waited their turns to unload at the factory, they shouted the news over the idling din of the one-lunger called Patsy D. "Women. Naked as jaybirds, they was," said one.

Much of the information was lost or misconstrued as it leapt from Cape Islander to Cape Islander, but the words *naked* and *women* were heard loud and clear.

With warp speed, the news travelled up the wharf to Austin and the fishery workers. By 1:15 the whole factory was abuzz. The delectable news was dissected across cutting and gutting tables and in the adjacent filet plant, and the driver of the freezer truck took it aboard along with the haddock and cod and pollack that it would carry onto the ferry and deliver to the mainland. Ferry workers spread the news from car to car to the captive audiences that` came and went from the island.

In short order, it reached the ears of Rebecca Prior. The middle-aged widow was the island's moral compass. A whitewashed Yankee, she had been born and raised on the island, but had spent the past 12 years in Lowell, Massachusetts, where her late husband had worked in a textile mill. She had "seen a few things" during her time in the big city and was determined that the evils of the larger world not be visited on her birthplace.

She had inserted herself onto every church committee and made sure that the hiring of new ministers was done in strict adherence to the tenets of the Baptist Convention. Her twelve-year absence, combined with her moral certainty, gave her an air of credibility and authority. Soon she had a vocal group of disciples throughout the village.

"If we don't stop it here and now, we're on the road to ruination," she told minister Thomas Idolson. Truth be told, Idolson could have cared less. At 49, he had lost his enthusiasm for religion. The seeds of doubt had been planted in this man of faith. But he was at that awkward age for a minister. Too young to retire, too

Beyond the Passage

old to change careers.

His lack of moral outrage allowed Rebecca to fill the vacuum, and she sprang into action on several fronts. She called an emergency meeting of the board of trustees. She called the RCMP to find out about the legalities of such a colony. She asked certain members of the congregation to visit the farm on the pretext of neighbourliness in order to gather evidence. She instructed the Wednesday-night prayer group to temporarily forsake the poor starving heathens of Africa and focus their prayers on eradicating this foothold of immorality and debauchery.

The Bible study discussions were definitive in nature, leaving little room for nuance or alternative interpretation. God himself obviously had frowned on nudity. It said so, right there in Genesis. Luckily there had been some off-the-rack fig leafs nearby to hide their shame.

Shame and nudity went together like fin and haddie, like Adam and Eve. And now the serpent had entered this Garden of Eden and God was not best pleased.

As the days and weeks passed, island fishermen seemed to be spending a lot more time fishing the waters adjacent to Charlie's old farm, an area not previously thought to be bountiful. Competition for the best view became so heated that the *Mary Ellen*, owned by Lemuel Nickerson, was rammed portside by the *Louise T*, captained by Merle Ossinger. Both men fell overboard and only quick action by one of "the colony" prevented disaster. The young lady was able to contact local fishermen via ship-to-shore, and soon Sherman Hoskin hauled the two combatants aboard his boat.

Rodney Lent, the local car service man, was working overtime because the undercarriages of several vehicles had been damaged. Some Sherlockian cynics attributed this spate of missing mufflers and tail pipes to the cratered road that ran down to the farm.

Suddenly, back issues of *National Geographic* and well-thumbed lingerie sections of the Simpson-Sears catalogue were no longer enough to satisfy the curiosity of young teenage boys. While these publications provided some clues, they didn't come close to solving the mysteries of the female anatomy.

69

Jim Prime

If you were observant, you would have seen these indomitable seekers of knowledge wander casually into the woods around sunset, after which they trudged through boot-sucking bogs and face slapping alder bushes to crouch in eager anticipation in the fir trees adjacent to the farm. Some even brought binoculars; those who didn't snuck closer to the farmhouse.

One unfortunate lad got his trouser leg snagged on the old barbed wire fence that surrounded the pasture behind the barn. One of the colony finally rescued him, as they rescued Kevin Boates, who had stepped into a gopher hole and turned his ankle. The very next evening Ray Garner fell from an oak tree at the corner of the property and dislocated his shoulder. Mechanics and doctors were doing a thriving business.

Sightings were now reported on a daily basis—at Curt's store or the post office. Fact and fiction blurred as stories were polished and salacious details added. Those with eye-witness details immediately attained celebrity status and others sought out their company.

When these young strangers came into town, they were extremely friendly, often engaging villagers in wide-ranging conversations on the wharf or at the store or on the steps of the IOOF Hall, where the youth of the town liked to gather and smoke unfiltered Export A cigarettes. From time to time the exotic visitors were seen knocking on village doors but when asked about it later, the homeowners were vague and evasive. This added another layer of intrigue for the rest of us. Were they recruiting—looking for liberal-minded individuals to join their free love cult? Many were convinced of it and others fervently prayed that they would come a calling on them.

Nevertheless, the rumours of orgies continued and some claimed that satanic rituals were being carried out in the moonlight. The spectre of human sacrifice was raised, although eventually dismissed. Anyone missing a cat or a dog immediately suspected the farm.

The village was a frenzied stew of raging hormones, fear, repressed desire, righteous indignation, and evangelical fervour. The

Beyond the Passage

population was polarized. There were the pros and the cons.

The situation reached a climax when Ed and Edith Stanton decided, after the Saturday-night dance at Lloyd's Hall, to give these newcomers a proper welcome. Let them know they understood the modern way of thinking.

Ed and Edith were only social drinkers, but unfortunately they were very social when drinking. After several improvised cocktails, they drove their '57 Chevy around the cove and turned up the road to the farm. The car lost its muffler within the first half mile and liquid was dripping from both the brake line and radiator.

Ed and Edith had read up on nudist colonies and had learned that voyeurs were not welcome. Only those totally committed to the cause of nature and freedom of expression were accepted.

It was in this spirit that they stopped just before the tree-lined road opened out into a grassy pasture. They proceeded to remove their clothes, tossing them into the back seat. Ed then urged the car along the worn grass track leading to the farmhouse. Lacking a muffler, the car approached like rolling thunder, and when they were in sight of the house, all six residents were peering from upstairs and downstairs windows.

He parked next to a dilapidated barn adjacent to the house and they exited the car unsteadily but proudly, as if making a statement. They were too drunk to notice the shrieks and hoots that greeted them as they staggered up the long expanse of uncut grass that led to the house.

"Welcome to the Islands," Ed shouted, extending his arms in a show of neighbourly acceptance. Without warning, all the lights in the house went out, leaving the overly-curious couple in complete darkness. They turned to leave but the drink and darkness had left them completely disoriented.

Edith stumbled into a patch of thistles and started hopping about in pain. Ed turned to help but stepped on the head of an abandoned hay rake. The handle sprung up, striking him in the most vulnerable part of his anatomy. There were moans and muffled curses and ear-piercing screams as they felt their way back to the car. Once inside the vehicle they examined their

71

Jim Prime

wounds before expressing in no uncertain terms their disappointment at the rude reception they'd received.

When they sobered up the next day they remembered little of what had happened but that didn't prevent them from describing events in tantalizing detail. Those who wanted to, believed their stories; those that thought it highly unlikely were nevertheless unable to erase the images from their minds for years after.

It was a seemingly endless summer of sunshine and possibilities and even the occasional foggy day did little to dampen spirits. Baseball continued to be played at Carmen's Field, a high plateau of land that offered a distant view of St. Mary's Bay down the third base line and a spectacular view of the Bay of Fundy just a sloping mile beyond first base.

As September arrived, the baseball season ended, tourists packed up and headed back home, and school reconvened. Seldom had essays on 'What I did last summer,' met with such scrutiny. The writing was replete with enough metaphors and other literary conventions to bring a wry smile to Mrs. Hooper's face. The English teacher was both impressed and aghast that one teenage boy had even suggested that he had "pole-vaulted into puberty" during the summer. Others had quite poetically opined about teenage angst and unrequited love.

And then one day the inevitable happened. The For Sale sign reappeared at the entrance to the farm road.

Its appearance had an immediate and varied impact on the citizenry. The church organized a Thanksgiving-style service in the middle of the week. The fishermen returned to their traditional fishing grounds. Teenage boys once again scoured the attics for old *National Geographics* and any mail order catalogue with a lingerie section. The doctor and the mechanic were no longer deluged with business. Tears were shed, fantasies shattered. The village returned to normal.

Much later we learned that the young people were part of a Cornell University study on the impact of environment on an individual's mental state. They had been conducting research, observing, mingling with the locals and collecting statistical and an-

Beyond the Passage

ecdotal data from random and highly confidential interviews.

We discovered this not by word of mouth but from the study that appeared in the *New England Journal of Psychiatry*, excerpts of which were reproduced in the *Digby Courier*. It was called the 'Aldertown Survey' to disguise the actual location and prevent embarrassment all round. But everyone knew it was the island.

Residents were not pleased. They knew that the behaviour of citizens had not been typical—in fact, anything but. It was the intrusion of outsiders that had caused them to act in such a bizarre fashion.

Nevertheless, the report was damning and the statistical breakdown and colour-coded bar chart that accompanied the article placed the village population into a range of mental health categories. For each and every disorder identified, anecdotal evidence was cited. Unlike most academic studies that gather cobwebs in university libraries, the dry treatise sold rather well, and a surprising number of copies found their way to Digby County.

Many of those surveyed read it with trepidation, fearing that their name would be included in bold print and accompanying footnotes citing examples of aberrant behaviour. But the researchers were discrete, using anonymous terms like case subject 1 and case subject 2 to ensure that privacy was maintained.

In addition to a variety of other more nuanced categories, the report suggested that the island was home to one idiot and one lunatic. Despite earnest and often heated arguments down at the general store, no consensus was ever reached as to which was which.

Jim Prime

The cat burglar

The laptop screen went pitch-black and remained that way for several minutes. Then there was a flicker of light and the camera quickly panned to an opening door.

A man in sneakers and black trousers entered, switching on the overhead light before closing the door behind him. The lens followed his legs as he moved to a workbench that occupied the opposite wall. The camera abruptly lurched and images blurred. When the frantic motion stopped, the focal point was higher and she could see the entire enclosure, top to bottom. There were rakes and shovels leaning against the wall and a lawnmower in the corner, half-covered by a tarp.

The man's back was to the camera. He reached into his large coat pocket and extracted a bulging handful which he tossed on the bench top. He moved to the left and sat on a stool, affording the camera a clear view of the work surface. Jewellery was divided into neat little piles—brooches, bracelets, necklaces, a mound of rings —all sparkling in the light of the naked bulb.

The man shimmied his stool closer and the scraping noise must have caused the videographer to flinch and retreat, because there was another brief interlude of darkness, followed by an extreme close-up of a rusty Valvoline oil can. Then the images blurred as the camera shook up and down, as if its user was having a sudden attack of nerves.

Jim and I have had our cat for 12 years now and we couldn't have hoped for a better companion. It may make non-cat people cringe to hear this, but Sophie really is part of the family. She's what you'd call an indoor-outdoor cat. We hadn't planned it that way, we knew the statistics that show that indoor cats live longer

Beyond the Passage

because they aren't exposed to the dangers that outdoor cats confront daily—battles with other cats, careless drivers, disease, fleas, and so on. But she got out one day when she was still a kitten and she took such delight in her surroundings—the grass, the chirping birds, spiders, you name it—that we decided it would be cruel to keep her inside on beautiful summer days.

We naively thought we could restrict her outdoor time. Boy, were we wrong! She wanted out on sunny days, rainy days, even on days when the snow was up to our living-room window sill.

Aside from a recent rash of break-ins several streets over, our subdivision is pretty quiet and peaceful. People look after each other and tolerate their pets. As for traffic, Sophie has become street wise over the years.

I don't want to give the idea that our little, grey, long-haired girl doesn't like to stay in sometimes, because she does, especially as she gets older. She loves to curl up with Jim and me as we watch TV, and often sleeps at the end of our bed. But it seems that when she's in, she wants out and when she's out, she wants in.

We often wondered where she went during her daily walkabouts. Once in a while we'd come upon her two streets over, or hear that she had visited a neighbour's deck, but there was a lot of time unaccounted for. Especially in the evenings, when she went for her final foray of the day.

One day recently, I was at my monthly book club, Loosely Bound. The book selection was *Rockbound,* about a Newfoundland veterinarian.

As often happens, our conversation took a detour. My friend Susan Surette-Draper happened to mention that a year earlier she and her husband had purchased a cat cam, a little digital camera that attaches to a cat's collar. This one was reasonably priced, she said, because she didn't opt for the night vision feature. She said that it was fun watching what their cat got up to in the run of a day, although lately the novelty had worn off and they had tucked the camera away somewhere.

I asked if she was interested in selling and, to make a long story short, we struck a deal.

Jim Prime

I was pretty excited when I brought it home and couldn't wait for Jim to see it. He loves gadgets. This one wasn't top of the line because of the night vision thing, but it did have a 110-degree, ul-tra-wide lens and some other cool add-ons.

I bought new batteries—it takes two heavy-duty AAs—cleaned the lens, and carefully attached it to Sophie's collar, according to the instructions. The battery life in 'constant record' mode was two and half hours. It also had a motion activated setting wherein it would stop recording if the cat stopped moving for more than 30 seconds, like if she had a nap or something.

It was a Wednesday night, which meant that Jim wouldn't be home until very late. He always had to work late on Wednesdays. Something about weekly inventory. It was already seven thirty and there was less than an hour of daylight left.

I considered waiting for the next day so that Jim could join in the fun, but finally decided to give the gizmo a trial run right away. Sophie rarely stayed out more than a couple of hours, so I decided to just leave it on continuous record. I adjusted the camera to the recommended angle for a cat her size and switched it on.

As I watched her trot down the driveway, I confess I felt a bit like a proud mother sending her child off to school for the first time.

She paused at the end of the drive, disappearing behind our bor-der hedge for a minute or so. Then she reappeared and crossed the street—I swear she looked both ways first—and went across the Hennigar's lawn before disappearing into the woods behind their house.

I have to say that I awaited her return with great anticipation. I was finally going to see what our little girl got up to when she was away from home. I couldn't wait to share all this with Jim.

Sure enough, in a little over two hours I heard her familiar scratch at the screen door. I let her in and she went directly to her food dish.

While she was eating, I removed the camera and attached it by cable to my laptop. I sat at the kitchen table like a little kid watch-ing her first Bugs Bunny cartoon.

The quality of the recording impressed me. The images were

76

Beyond the Passage

sharp and distinct. At first the camera showed the pavement as she was leaving the doorway, then she stopped and looked back at me. I was viewing myself through her eyes, although I'm told that cats see in black and white. I now could see that she had stopped to sniff the garbage bag Jim had left by the hedge before heading off to work.

It was everything I had seen her do from the kitchen window, but from her own viewpoint. Extremely cool!

Once she entered the woods, I kind of lost my bearings for a while. Then she was headed up a street via the ditch, taking a shortcut through a culvert before emerging again into the fading sunlight.

She spotted another cat—another female named Trixie from the Crossman place. They locked eyes and the fur went up on Trixie's back and she spat toward the camera.

After a brief standoff, Sophie continued her trek, glancing back at her rival a couple of times. At one point she stopped to scratch vigorously—she doesn't have fleas, just dry skin—and the camera shook as if it was being wielded by one of those artsy directors, like in the *Blair Witch Project*.

Another long, uneventful stretch, and then she crossed another street and entered a copse of trees. She stopped and must have sat down. For the next few minutes I got a close-up view of her lower anatomy as she tended to her toilette. She repeated this a few more times in the next few minutes.

She must have heard a squirrel chatter, because the camera angled up toward a tall maple tree. I couldn't see the squirrel but I did see the leaves moving. She was still for quite a while as she watched the little creature, then she stalked slowly and deliberately toward it.

The squirrel was too savvy for her, however, and soon Sophie resumed her walk, coming out of the woods and passing through a gap in a chain-link fence. At this point I had no idea where she was. There was a row of houses, but none I recognized. No one knows the backs of people's houses, I guess. Very disorienting.

I'd been watching the small screen for a little over an hour and

Jim Prime

the novelty had already worn off a bit. I now understood why Susan had been so willing to part with this device. Still, I was glad to have done it and didn't begrudge the money. Jim always worried when Sophie went out in the evenings and this might put his mind at ease. She was an explorer, all right, but never got herself into any real danger.

I picked up the new book that our group had selected for discussion at our next meeting. With Jim gone, Wednesday nights were the perfect time to read without interruptions. Every so often I'd glance at the laptop just to monitor Sophie's progress.

She examined some dog poop on a driveway, started a butterfly into flight, sat under a rose bush for a while and then approached a small outbuilding. I was about to resume my reading when she headed directly for the shed as if on a mission. It was obviously familiar to her.

As she neared the wall, the camera revealed a small opening where the shed sat on a cinder-block foundation. She ducked under the wall, and everything went black.

My laptop screen remained blank for a good half hour. I smiled because I was sure Sophie was sleeping. No wonder she had the energy to keep us up at night with her shenanigans.

Then the scene was bathed in light and I saw a man enter the shed. He sat there on a stool, writing in a notebook, as if he were taking inventory of goods on the bench.

I didn't know what to do. I was worried about Sophie, of course, but there was something else. I suddenly wished that Jim were home.

When I exhausted every other explanation but criminal activity, I called the RCMP. I felt a bit awkward explaining it to the dispatcher but she was all business, as if this kind of thing was routine, which I'm sure it wasn't, not in New Minas. She asked for our address and said that a cruiser would be along shortly.

She was true to her promise: within five minutes a police car pulled into our driveway and two young officers got out and walked briskly toward the house.

I opened the front door before they had a chance to knock. "I'm

Beyond the Passage

Glenna," I said. "Thanks for coming so quickly."

I invited them in and they sat on either side of me at the kitchen table.

We all looked at the screen. The video was still playing. Infuriatingly, Sophie was still grooming herself behind a box with 'Cashmere, You deserve a soft touch' written on the side. Since the light was on, we assumed the burglar was still in the room.

The officers watched with great interest, taking the whole thing very seriously.

"And you really have no idea where this might be?" the taller of the two men said.

"No, I really don't," I said. "If Sophie would just look at him again."

"Probably scared," the shorter man said. "Wants to stay hidden. It's a matter of which will win out—her fear or her curiosity."

The words were barely out of his mouth when the man came into view again, first partially and then full on, still from the back. He was dressed entirely in black and wore a toque.

The man reached into an inside jacket pocket and pulled out a candy bar—a Crispy Crunch, I think it was. The moment he began opening the wrapper the camera steadied, locked on the man, just as it had earlier when Sophie was watching the squirrel.

I realized that the sound of the wrapper was probably the same as that made when I opened a bag of Temptations, Sophie's favourite treat. It had always been a sure way to get her attention. if she'd been out too long, for instance, we'd stand on the deck and shake one of those bags and she'd appear, like magic.

She must have meowed, because the man's head jerked around. He rose from the stool and walked toward the camera, a smile of recognition on his face. He was now looking directly into the camera.

To my horror, I saw that it was Jim. My jaw fell open. A thousand thoughts raced through my head.

The police hadn't noticed my distress. They were busy scribbling notes on his appearance.

Jim's hand reached toward Sophie. The screen blurred, there

79

Jim Prime

was a brief fade to black and then grey as house lights illuminated shadowy outlines of trees and bushes.

After a deep intake of breath and a few false starts, I stammered out my revelation to the officers.

Very calmly and precisely, they asked me to think very hard about where this might be. I didn't answer. I think I was in shock.

"Do you have a shed on the property?" the smaller man said.

"No, no we don't."

And then it dawned on me.

"Our neighbours do," I managed to say. "They've been away for three weeks on a trip. They aren't due back for another two weeks."

I hesitated before adding, "We have a key."

I must have been having a kind of out-of-body experience because I could hear myself talking in a monotone, as if I was some dispassionate witness to a crime.

"Where?" the larger officer said. It was now obvious that he was the man in control. His voice was no longer gentle.

I led them to the side door and out onto our deck. Sophie ran past us into the house before the spring-loaded aluminum door could swing shut.

My hand trembling, I pointed toward the shed that the Wilders had installed the previous summer.

Within seconds, the officers were standing on either side of the shed door, guns drawn. "Police," they yelled in unison.

"Open up!" the younger man added. "And come out slowly, with your hands above your head."

Even in my shattered state of mind I had the passing impression that he'd always wanted to say that.

There was a slight delay, and I could imagine the panic that Jim was experiencing. Then he flung the door open and emerged with his hands up.

As they were handcuffing him, Jim glanced toward the house and saw me standing there, my hands covering my mouth. I could actually see him wither, his entire body seeming to deflate.

The police escorted him to their car and deposited him in the

Beyond the Passage

back seat. One of the officers returned to the deck to tell me they'd be in touch. Then they left.

Only the chirping of crickets broke the silence. I was completely alone.

A wave of nausea passed through me and I collapsed into our red Adirondack chair, not knowing what to do or who to turn to. Sophie had collared a criminal and that criminal was my own husband.

Suddenly she jumped onto my lap and began kneading my skirt with her claws. She turned in a complete circle and lay down.

I stroked her repeatedly from head to tail as she purred her approval and curled into a tight ball. Within minutes, her purring had ceased. She expelled one last long sigh and fell asleep.

Cats are such a comfort, especially when you're on your own like I am.

Jim Prime

Incident at The Beaverbrook

It's a steaming hot day in the late spring of 1978. You check into the Lord Beaverbrook Hotel in Fredericton at 4:30 on a Tuesday, feeling tired and grubby after the five-hour drive from Dartmouth.

You take the elevator up to your fifth floor room, put your suitcase on the bed and go to the window. You look out at Queen Street and regret that you didn't request the river view. You consider calling the front desk to change rooms, but can't be bothered.

You go through your well-practised travel routine. You switch on the TV for some background noise, unpack your suit bag and hang two shirts, a sports jacket and grey dress pants in the narrow closet. You place your toiletries—razor, shave cream, toothbrush and toothpaste—on the bathroom counter. You avoid putting anything into the dresser because you've left items at hotels all across the Maritimes. Instead you stack them in plain sight on a chair by the door.

You find the plasticized menu next to the phone and consider ordering room service. Instead, you take a quick shower, turning the dial gradually from warm to cold and emerge after ten minutes refreshed and re-energized.

The room is stuffy so you slide the air conditioner knob to Cool and set the speed to High. You pull on your jeans and T-shirt and go down to the lobby, where you grab a complimentary copy of the *Globe and Mail* from the stand next to the reception desk.

The lobby is well-appointed, with tasteful groupings of chairs and low tables. Curved marble staircases descend from each side of the upper lobby, meeting at a wide marble landing. The railing tops are highly-polished oak and the sides feature an intricate maple leaf motif in black wrought iron. Rich, dark pillars and

Beyond the Passage

brushed copper coats of arms reflect the stately elegance of another era.

Your eyes are drawn upwards to the high, vaulted ceiling. A massive chandelier illuminates upper and lower lobbies, its sparkling facets bathing both levels in light.

You notice a discrete plaque near the entrance. It informs you that the Lord Beaverbrook Hotel opened on August 13, 1948, with Sir Max Aiken himself—Winston Churchill's one-time right hand man—in attendance.

The Lord Beaverbook has three dining options: a steak house, a regular restaurant and a pub located just off the lobby. After a brief moment of indecision, you decide on the pub.

Unlike the bright lobby, it is sombre and softly lit, exuding gravity and importance. It's not hard to imagine Sir Max and Sir Winston discussing world events over Scotch and cigars near the large fireplace that occupies the far end of the spacious room.

In fact political drama is still playing out every day within these panelled walls, albeit without worldwide implications. Premier Richard Hatfield's cabinet have lately come under public scrutiny for spending overly long, overly liquid lunches drafting acts of law. You smile. Legislation by libation. *Not a bad line*, you think. *I may use that someday*.

UNB professors use the Beveridge room as a late-afternoon retreat, grateful for a respite from the unseemly enthusiasms of youth. A party of retired profs of various ages, conditions, and areas of expertise augment their number.

It occurs to you that "party" of retired professors hardly seems like the appropriate collective noun—perhaps tenure of profs might be better. Most seem to be wearing some variety of corduroy sports jacket, many with patches at the elbow, and narrow, wrinkled ties. They smoke pipes and cigarettes and nod knowingly. The younger ones are fashionably unkempt. The rest are simply unkempt. The politicians and professors are all male.

The bar itself is long and imposing, taking up most of one wall before bending elegantly around a corner toward the lobby entrance. A brass rail provides a place for elbows to rest. The stools

Jim Prime

are wooden with high backs. Behind the bar, the barman is dressed in a white shirt and wears a tartan bow tie.

The bar is generously stocked, and features the finest brands of scotch, rye, rum, gin and vodka. The inventory is doubled in the large mirror behind the bar that also allows you to check out the room without turning your head.

There is something different about the bar this evening. Unfamiliar sounds cause you to scan the mirror for their source. These are not the conspiratorial murmurs of politicians or the self-assured pontificating of academics. No, those conversations reach your ears as indecipherable mumbles. These are young voices. Young female voices. Sporadic ripples of laughter. Sounds that these venerable walls choose to reflect rather than absorb.

Heads turn. Disapproving looks are passed, unheeded by the interlopers.

You ask the bartender about it. He says that the hotel is attempting to attract a younger clientele and have promoted Tuesday nights as College nights. "Meet me at the Beav" say the inviting full page ads in the campus newspapers. Special prices on drinks if you show your UNB or St. Thomas University ID. And, he adds with a shake of his head, an extended closing time. If the promotion catches on, there is even talk of bringing in entertainers, albeit quiet and tasteful ones, Simon and Garfunkelish in tone.

His exaggerated eye rolls and general demeanour make it obvious that the bartender disapproves—and assumes that you do, too. You don't.

You order a second draft of dark British ale and move to a table in proximate range of the university crowd. And why not? After all, you're barely out of university yourself.

While the other co-eds at the table are chugging their cheap beer, you strike up a conversation with the young lady closest to you. Turns out she's a graduate student in political science with a double major in journalism. She's from Bathurst and has a delightful French accent. You tell her that you have done some writing but the topic quickly turns to politics.

She talks about the need for a radical shift from the old ways—

Beyond the Passage

perhaps even two New Brunswicks, one for the English and one for the French. You agree in that hypocritical way one does when possibilities take precedence over principles.

You are invited to join the table, which you do. Four females and one male. They introduce themselves with nods and first names that you immediately forget. The guy is in engineering, the girls are all arts students of one variety or other. Although the age gap is not great, you are surprised at how naïve the students are. Except for Denise.

After a few more beers, the other four excuse themselves and go outside to smoke a joint, leaving you alone with the radical poly sci student.

She looks around and gestures expansively. "Just look around you. I see at least six government MLAs, including four ministers. And all four ministers have been involved in some sort of scandal —sex, drugs, alcohol. I mean these are our leaders? It's disgusting for grown men to act this way. We need a return to decency."

You attempt to match her level of contempt with head shakes and disparaging curse words and hope that she buys it. She likes the NDP and sees them as the voice of her generation. It's a friendly, bantering conversation. You sense that she likes you even if she doesn't respect your political insights.

The others come back, noticeably more mellow. Their return reminds you that you have to leave. You have an early appointment at the Department of Education. You excuse yourself and go out into the lobby.

Denise follows. You tell her how much you enjoyed her company. She invites you to call her next time you're in Fredericton and gives you her floor number at Marshall D'Avary Hall. She gives you a little peck on the cheek and disappears back into the lounge.

Feeling the effects of the Guinness, you move deliberately across the quiet lobby, this space that exudes such dignity, such refinement, such sophistication, and take the elevator back to your room. A blast of heat strikes you when you open the door. The windows have been closed and it's stinking hot. The ancient A/C has been blowing warm air for hours. You turn the knob all the way to Cold

85

Jim Prime

but there is no change. You wind open the two small windows that aren't sealed, but it makes no difference.

You strip to your boxers and lie on the bed. The sweat pours off you. You remove the blanket and lie on the sheets, hoping they may cool you, but they don't.

You suddenly realize that there's a mini-fridge in the room. You remove your shorts, sit on the floor in front of it and open the door. You sit there for a full five minutes before noticing that it's un-plugged. You've been sitting in front of a dead appliance.

You decide that what you need is a cross breeze. You grab a plastic waste basket from the bathroom and prop open the door. You finally feel a waft of coolish air, but before you can enjoy it the rounded waste basket pops out and the door slams shut. You try this two more times. Each time it stays in place for a minute and then squirts out.

You peek your head out into the deserted hallway and notice a room service trolley outside the room across the hall. The trolley would be ideal for propping open the door. You stretch your arm out to grab it, but it's just beyond your reach.

You wedge the wastebasket in place once more and take another step into the hall, your hand losing contact with the door handle for a split second. As you grasp the handle of the trolley, the spring-loaded door slams shut behind you with the finality of a prison cell.

You are now standing naked in the hallway. Your heart sinks, colliding with your stomach which is lurching upwards. At last you feel cold—cold panic.

Frantically, you look around. There is no one in sight. You quickly weigh your options. The trolley holds a large stainless steel serving platter, complete with a domed oval cover. Someone has ordered the full hot meal. You consider the notion of placing the cover over your lower anatomy and going down to the front desk for another key. The idea conjures up a bizarre image that you might find humorous if it were happening to anyone but you.

Nevertheless, the idea persists; you see yourself meeting some late night stragglers on the elevator and removing the cover with a

Beyond the Passage

flourish and the accompanying word, *Voila*!

You see the royal blue table cloth on the trolley and give quiet thanks to Lord Beaverbrook for supplying it. You grab it as if it was an Armani suit you discovered in the bin at Frenchies.

Sadly, it is not a large table cloth, enough to cover your front or your back but not both. You try to stretch it and re-arrange it but every strategic positioning fails. You wrap it around your front.

You take a deep breath. You contemplate the domed cover. Its use no longer seems so bizarre. Your internal monologue argues against it, but you grab it anyway, holding it out as a shield as you move down the hallway.

Your one piece of attire, your watch, tells you it's 12:55 a.m. Surely everyone is asleep at this hour on a week night, in Fredericton, a Baptist town famous for its early to bed, early to rise work ethic.

You suddenly become a field marshal, mapping out a strategy that will take you from your present vulnerable position to your front desk target and back to your bunker. It's a minefield but you think you can do it.

You consider the elevator but dismiss the idea. Being trapped naked in such a confined space sends shivers up your all-too-exposed spine. You decide that the stairs are your safest option and, looking furtively both ways, you duck through the exit door and make your way down the five flights.

You reach the upper lobby without incident. There is no one in sight. You walk on tip toes to the beautiful curved stairway and make your way down, as nonchalantly as possible. You fight the feeling that you are making your grand entrance at the ball. Your face is bright red.

You send up a silent prayer that the night clerk is male. You peek out from behind a pillar and are delighted to see that your prayer has been answered.

You rush up to the startled young man and blurt out your situation: "Locked out of room 505, key please."

To his credit, he hesitates only a moment before retrieving the duplicate from a round pigeon hole on the wall behind him and

Jim Prime

handing it to you. So far so good.

You turn quickly and retreat toward the staircase. The lobby is completely empty. You are practically home free. You begin your ascent when suddenly the door to the lounge pub swings open.

You suddenly remember about the extended closing time. It's 1 a.m. The lounge disgorges a mixture of tipsy politicians and professors. Behind them are the university students.

As you turn to run, your table cloth snags on the wrought iron rail. You turn back to retrieve it. Quickly remembering your vulnerable state, you place the warming cover over your lower regions. Everyone is looking at you. You lock eyes with Denise, who looks back in horror.

You flee, leaving your rear guard exposed, and take the stairs two at a time. You hear a piercing wolf whistle, followed by a variety of disparaging remarks interspersed with laughter. The laughter echoes in your ears all the way back to your room.

Your hand is shaking but finally get the key in the hole and turn it. You enter your room. The door slams behind you and you lean against it. After a few minutes you discard your shield and remove the cloth.

Only then do you feel the full enormity of the situation. You wonder if enormity is the correct word and quickly confirm that it DAMN WELL is.

You know that you can never return to this hotel. Perhaps you can never return to this city. Moncton, perhaps, Saint John, sure, why not? Your indiscretions there would scarcely be noticed. But not the "City of Stately Elms."

You hear a distant siren and hold your breath until it fades. You feel an unwanted kinship with the scandal-ridden Hatfield cabinet. You lie on the bed in the fetal position, shattered and perspiring and eventually you fall into a fitful sleep.

The next morning you go downstairs for an early check-out. You loiter a discrete distance from the counter, waiting for the night clerk's shift to end. Finally his replacement arrives and they have a brief exchange before he leaves.

She is a prim, middle-aged lady with a severe hairdo. Pleasant,

Beyond the Passage

but all business. You pay by credit card and turn to leave.

You walk quickly toward the brass trimmed glass doors but, just before you reach them, you hear a stifled laugh. You swing around to confront her, but when you do, her face is serene and composed.

Jim Prime

A duck's dilemma

It was one of the saddest sights I've ever seen, probably a metaphor for something, although I'm not sure what. I've thought about it a lot, even though it happened about eight years ago now.

I was driving to Halifax from the Valley and had reached the Bicentennial Highway, the last, or maybe the first, leg of Highway 102. I was heading into the city for an appointment at the Department of Education. I was still a book rep for a publishing house at the time, and I had an appointment at 9:00 with the Director of Curriculum, a fairly big deal.

I didn't exactly love my job, but it paid reasonably well and I had a wife and two kids to support. Besides, I had been working in publishing for about thirty years at that point, and it was too late to change professions. That particular ship had sailed. My goal was to hang on for a few more years until I could escape into retirement.

The BiHi is a high-traffic area, one of a precious few entry points onto the peninsula where Halifax sits. In the 1970s, as the population of our capital city grew, the Department of Highways put in a four-foot-high concrete divider to separate incoming and outgoing traffic. The barrier is about two feet wide at the top and curves out to maybe four feet at the base.

It was about 8:05 and I was making good time. Traffic was brisk but moving along well.

I always like to be early, so I can grab a coffee, sit in my car and go over my notes before talking to a key educator. Experience had taught me that it pays off. You need to appear to know what you're talking about when you deal with people at this level—the latest buzz words, factoids from the latest research into how we learn,

Beyond the Passage

just enough to seem on top of things.

I hated kowtowing to these people. Sometimes I felt like saying, "This is the same theory that was around ten years ago, under a different name." But sometimes you have to do what you have to do.

I had just passed the Bayer's Lake turnoff and was listening to a local radio station, one of those open-mouth shows that we don't get in the Valley. I seem to recall they were talking about chickens, specifically whether Haligonians should be allowed to raise them within city limits. In any case, it was a lively discussion and I was enjoying the back and forth from callers.

I was moving along at maybe 75 kph, travelling in the far left lane next to the concrete median. I could see the city in the distance, the outline of buildings and occasional glimpses of the harbour.

All of a sudden, out of the corner of my eye, I saw a flash of movement up ahead. It was one of those double-take situations. I really didn't know what it was at first.

As I got closer, it became all too obvious what it was. It's an image that is burned into me, perhaps, as I said earlier because it's some kind of metaphor.

It was a procession of ducks. Well, one mother duck and eight mottled little ducklings following her single file. They were walking between the concrete and the yellow line that ran parallel to it, a width of maybe three or four feet. And I mean to tell you they were walking—waddling, I guess you'd call it since they were ducks. The mother was going a mile a minute, those little webbed feet that had evolved to paddle effortlessly across water moving up and down on the hard pavement, and those little guys were keeping up with her, every last one of them.

They were in a predicament. They couldn't escape to the left because of the concrete barrier. They couldn't go right because of the heavy traffic.

I slowed as much as I could and looked down at those ducks— talk about determined! That mother had a goal and that was to get those ducklings out of this man-made crisis. God knows how they got there. There are lakes all around. It had to have happened be-

Jim Prime

fore the traffic started to build and by the time she realized she had made a mistake it was too late.

I looked around me and I'm not sure too many other people even noticed the ducks. As I went by I looked down at them but they didn't give a sideways glance at me.

It occurred to me in a flash that I should stop and scoop them into my van, but by the time I formed the thought, it was too late. There were cars right behind me, so it would almost certainly have caused a fender-bender at least, and probably worse.

I continued to watch them in my rear view mirror for as long as I could until other cars hid them from view. And then I looked ahead and the city of Halifax was still looming in the distance.

I looked at my odometer and wrote down the number. Then I grabbed my bag phone—that's what we had back then; sounds ancient now—with the notion of calling someone. But who? Was this something that deserved a 911 call? Probably not. SPCA? I had no idea how to get in touch with them, especially at 8:15 in the a.m. RCMP? I even thought of calling in to the radio talk show; it wouldn't be too much of a segue from their chicken topic and I did have their number because they repeated it every fifteen minutes or so.

In the end I did none of those things. I took the Bayer's Road exit into the city. This was where the median ended. I determined that it was three and a half miles from the ducks' location to possible escape.

I got myself a coffee at the Tim's drive-thru at the corner of Young and Robie, proceeded downtown to Brunswick Street and parked across from the Trade Mart Scotia Square, where the Department of Education is located. I pumped some loonies into the meter and sat there, drinking the coffee and thinking about those little ducks and the fix they were in.

Finally, at ten to nine I went into the Department and waited for the secretary to summon me to my appointment. God, I would rather have been almost anywhere. Of course, that applied to most if not all of my appointments, but today it was even worse. But sacrifices have to be made, and so I smiled and tried to be as charming

Beyond the Passage

as possible, all the while feeling like Willie Loman in *Death of a Salesman.*

When I drove home later that day on the BiHi heading toward the Valley, I took the Bayer's Lake exit and doubled back, just to see if I could spot those ducks. I saw nothing—no signs of ducks, living or dead. Maybe a good sign. Maybe someone called someone who stopped traffic and allowed those ducks to get back to the other side of the road. Who knows?

I didn't see anything about it on *Live at Five* or in the *Herald* and you'd think they would be all over a human interest fluff piece like this. Tailor-made for ratings, I would have thought.

I've been retired for a few years now, and glad of it. Out of the rat race, off the treadmill. No more forced smiles and phony small talk. No more awkward dinners with key customers with whom I had nothing in common. The kids are grown and married and living in San Diego and Kentville.

I sometimes think back over my career in sales. It was good at first, then only tolerable, and at the end I felt like a martyr, I admit it. But you know, of all those memories over a 36-year career in publishing—all those sales conferences, all those teachers conventions and book displays and nights on the road in god knows where—I still think mostly of that mother duck and those eight little ducklings, walking along that hard pavement with no relief in sight.

Strange, I know. Like I say, I think it's a hell of a metaphor for something, although I'll be damned if I know what.

Jim Prime

The rights of spring

The prehistoric giant moved silently through the dark waters of the Gulf, heading north. Her stocky body wasn't designed for speed and she moved at a lumbering pace, but with purpose. Seen from the air the black mass could easily have been mistaken for a shallow reef, an impression furthered by the white barnacles and sea lice that encrusted large areas of her enormous head.

At her side, under her left pectoral fin, swam her four-month-old calf. The two right whales moved with the precision of synchronized swimmers, the youngster mimicking her mother's every fall and rise, each undulation and subtle shift. The calf was still nursing, draining the mother's energy and slowing their progress.

The calf was small only in relation to its 50-foot-long mother. From nose to fluke it already measured 19 feet and was growing rapidly. Its body was pale grey and the white patches of callused skin hadn't yet developed the hard protrusions of parasites that marked the mother.

The pair was approaching the mouth of the Bay of Fundy, on their way to the feeding grounds near Brier Island, Nova Scotia. Their journey had begun weeks before, off the coast of Florida. The warm southern waters were ideal for calving, but food there was not abundant and both mammals desperately needed to eat. The cow's fat reserves, already diminished from the sparse diet, had been further depleted by the arduous swim. The calf was still nursing, draining her energy and slowing their progress.

They had fallen miles behind the rest of the small pod, but the route was familiar and the banquet that she knew awaited them pushed the mother whale forward. Once in the bay, they could rest and gorge themselves in the copepod-rich inland waters. A ready

Beyond the Passage

supply of plankton and krill would soon satisfy their hunger.

Cruising just feet beneath the surface, the mother whale felt the proximity of the shore and was energized. She abandoned the maternal caution that had dictated her speed and route, and plunged ahead at eight miles per hour.

The calf sensed her mother's excitement and struggled to match her tempo. It was an exuberant sprint to the finish line, and the goal—the safe and bountiful feeding grounds of the Scotian Shelf.

Then came a sickening thud that drove the mother's body forward and down. A sharp wedge of steel had struck her right side, midway between fin and tail, ripping through flesh, blubber, and sinew before sawing across the backbone.

Instinctively, she dove, 50 feet, 75, feet 100 feet, entrails escaping from the wound.

Finally her descent slowed and then ceased. Stunned, she looked about for her calf, but she was nowhere in sight.

The blow had opened a deep, vertical gash and she fought to maintain her balance. Above her the huge oil tanker passed, its shadow throwing a veil over the horrible drama playing out below. The large propellers churned the bloody waters and within minutes light from the surface, tinted red as it passed through the scarlet filter, returned.

Suddenly, the calf appeared at her side, trembling and confused. The mother's body had taken the full impact of the blow, shielding the young one and pushing her out of harm's way. She nuzzled against the undamaged side of her mother, unaware of her desperate plight.

The ocean around her was now a darker red as billows of blood enveloped both creatures. The bow of the double-hulled tanker had sliced through layers of fat and muscle, shattering the rib cage and exposing a two-foot section of backbone.

Somehow, the whale summoned the energy to dive again, internal organs now trailing from the fatal wound. The calf followed in her wake.

Wracked with convulsions, the broken and dying whale somehow willed herself forward. She was acutely aware of the calf at

Jim Prime

her side, and the maternal instinct won out over the urge to give up.

For more than an hour, she continued to advance in frenetic bursts, the traumatized calf in tow. The spasms of movement were interrupted by periods of calm while the exhausted mammal floated on the current, its fluke raised as a kind of sail. Then she would begin again, her erratic movements transitioning into death throes. The excruciating tableau continued for more than an hour as they came under the tidal pull of Grand Passage.

Within minutes sharks appeared, attracted by the obscene chum of blood and entrails. They tore viciously at her side, ripping away large chunks of flesh, and turning the waters a deeper crimson.

The desperate calf pushed against the pectoral fin, trying to nudge her mother forward, out of danger. The water grew shallower and the sharks backed off, their mouths streaming blood.

The whale gave one last shudder and was dead. She continued to move shoreward, her body now borne along by the incoming tide, before being drawn into an underwater gully that led to the beach.

The young whale was comforted by the renewed speed and the way its mother glided effortlessly ahead. She continued to prod her side, puzzled by the lack of response. She followed the drifting corpse as it passed through the narrow channel.

The powerful spring tide carried the mother past jutting sand bars and over an extended bed of rock until the bottom turned to sand and began to angle up to the beach. There, in the detritus of the high-water mark, it finally came to rest.

Some twenty yards behind, the smaller whale ceased its forward motion as her belly touched the stony bottom. Alerted to danger, she tried to pivot in the narrow channel. The tide was turning and the water in the tight canal was rapidly growing shallow. Within minutes she would be grounded alongside her mother.

With growing panic, the youngster struggled, her instinct for survival overcoming the bond with her mother. Finally turned toward the open water, she lowered her muscular fluke and rapidly arched it upward, forcing her body across the smooth rock bed.

Beyond the Passage

Once free, she swam at full speed until she was back in deep water.

Only then did she halt her retreat, pause as if collecting her thoughts, and surface briefly for air before submerging. She then swam back and forth parallel to the shore, rising and diving, slowly at first and then with increasing agitation.

The dead whale had settled on its side, its white, almost luminescent underbelly buffeted by the waves. The shark attack had left deep gouges in the massive body, suggestive of the frantic chisel strokes of some mad sculptor.

Humans tend to anthropomorphize animals, perhaps because doing so makes them somehow more relatable. In cartoons, pigs talk, dogs walk on two legs and bears wear hats and bow ties.

The nobility and mystery of whales makes them difficult to humanize but we do try. The same right whales return to the Bay of Fundy every year, and every year hundreds of elementary school children go on whale watch field trips to see them breach and blow and seemingly perform for boatloads of delighted onlookers. It's an awe-inspiring experience.

This experience often moves the children to learn more—about the whales' habitat, their migration habits, and the fact that for many reasons, man-made and natural, they are endangered, with less than 400 northern right whales left in the world.

Some classes even adopt a whale, receiving a certificate of adoption in exchange for a donation to conservation. NOAA charts the movements of each whale and carefully catalogues them. Each receives a code number from NOAA and other scientific organizations.

But they also have regular names, based on their unique and easily recognizable markings. Names like Snowball and Queenie, cute kids' names.

On the other side of the island, Josh Garron stood in his sun porch and scanned the western sky for tomorrow's weather, but the fog hung offshore, unwilling to reveal much information. Following his divorce, he had decided to move back home. There was nothing to keep him in the city and, in any case, too many painful memories.

Jim Prime

The family home bordered the cove and he watched as the tide slowly retreated across the flats, revealing glistening new real estate. The seascape was gradually becoming a landscape of mud, sand, scattered tide pools, and seaweed-covered rock formations. At the head of the cove, the high water mark was clearly distinguishable by a curving line of kelp, seaweed, and assorted flotsam and jetsam.

Josh adjusted his binoculars to watch the snipes as they retreated with the waves, only to form an advance guard for the next diminished surge. Their quest for bloodworms and other invertebrates was urgent and their long slender bills pumped the mud like jackhammers.

Josh always found the cove comfortably predictable. The water would continue to ebb until it reached the rusting bell buoy adjacent to the government breakwater, languish there for awhile as if plotting its next move, and then advance once again. *Not a bad metaphor for my life*, he thought, taking another long, slow draught from the bottle of Ten Penny Ale.

He sometimes imagined the cove as a battlefield of a never-ending military campaign. In summer, fog frequently obscured his view, the swirling, leaden-grey mists hanging in the air like smoke from ten thousand muskets. But he always knew that behind the shroud the assault and withdrawal continued unabated. Fundy's tides—the highest in the world—would storm the beaches and lay siege for a short time, only to be beaten back.

After spending eleven years in the smog of Toronto, he found the smells of the cove intoxicating. When the tide was out, the air was redolent with the pungent mix of decay and rebirth that summer visitors found unpleasant but which he loved. When the basin was full, the rich mixture of brine and salt air was almost overpowering. It wasn't so much breathed in as it was absorbed into his body, permeating and enveloping him like some alien entity.

Not for the first time, he wondered how anyone could live far from the sea. It helped him to sleep at night and gave him a reason to wake in the morning. Even when a westerly breeze occasionally brought with it the aroma of rotting fish from the processing

Beyond the Passage

plant's gurry bin, he welcomed it.

There was a time when Josh had known every Cape Islander that came and went: The Alice 11, the Veronica, Banker's Mistress, the Two Sisters, the Elsie & Joan, and on and on and on. He had known the boats and the wives, daughters and girlfriends they'd been named for. He'd even slept with a few of them—one aboard the very boat that bore her name. It had been a true christening, complete with champagne.

He'd also known every skipper and crew member. He could tell by how low or high the returning boat was riding if it had been a good day or not.

Something caught his eye and he trained his binoculars on the bluff of land on the opposite side of the cove. A flock of seagulls was circling just above Roney's Point, a cliff that rose above Grand Passage. In turns they swooped out of sight behind the landfall and reappeared seconds later.

Unusual at this time of day, he thought. The fishermen had all returned and their boats were either tied up at the wharf or moored and bobbing gently at the entrance to the cove. There would be no bait for gulls to scavenge at this hour. Maybe a spill from the gurry bin at the R.L. Davis and Sons fish factory.

The gulls were becoming more agitated and their numbers were growing. This was more than a bag of drowned kittens or some fish guts. There was something there, something that didn't belong, something big. He decided to investigate.

He roused myself from the ancient, faded-red-to-pink chesterfield that was the centerpiece of the sun porch, pulled on his boots and headed out to the '89 International truck that he had bought second-hand at Beliveau Motors across the bay in Meteghan. The truck was originally forest green, but was now at least thirty percent body fill.

With the help of two vigorous pumps of the choke, it groaned to life on the second try and Josh headed down the dirt road that led around the cove. The late afternoon sun was falling fast and the streets of the village were deserted. Freeport was a typical fishing community—its inhabitants rose early and retired early.

99

Jim Prime

As he drew nearer, Josh saw that crows and a few hawks had joined the flock of seagulls. He parked the truck at the side of the road and crossed the road to peer over the side of the cliff.

There on the beach, half in the water, lay the steaming carcass of a right whale.

Josh made his way down the steep incline and onto the beach, the seagulls screaming indignantly as they took to the air. He walked slowly around the body, examining it from various angles.

The buildup of callosities on the head was as conclusive as a fingerprint. He thought of his daughter, now a successful artist. He thought of her love of nature and how it had inspired her to become a painter. He thought of a drawing she had made many years earlier, when she was in grade five.

It was a drawing of a whale, with the name Snowball painstakingly printed underneath. For months the picture had been taped to the refrigerator next to a certificate of adoption.

Josh looked out into the passage and saw a young whale diving and surfacing. He watched the whale for a long time, then slowly drove home through the darkened village.

Beyond the Passage

My internal monologue

A quintessential writer's study. The floor is knee-deep in crumpled sheets of paper. Bookcases groan under the weight of copies of Jim Prime books.

Sound of crickets chirping.

JIM
Wake up, brain.

BRAIN
What? Whattaya want?

JIM
I need an internal monologue by Friday.

BRAIN
Why?

JIM
Teacher says so.

BRAIN
Just tell her you had one. How'll she know the difference?

JIM
You don't understand. I need to read my internal monologue aloud to the class.

Jim Prime

BRAIN
Then it's hardly internal, is it?

JIM
Well, no, I suppose not.

BRAIN
Then I've given you a loophole, haven't I?

JIM
In theory, yes. But I don't think Susan, she's the instructor, is gonna buy it.

BRAIN
Hard ass, is she?

JIM
Dearest, most supportive person I know. Saint-like, really, and a brilliant writer in her own right. Full disclosure: I'll be reading this in her class. The problem is, some other people in the class have their internal monologues spoutin' off 24/7. I don't know how they get any sleep.
BRAIN
Makes you look bad, eh?

JIM
I feel intense pressure.

BRAIN
So you need the internal monologist.

JIM
I do.

BRAIN

Beyond the Passage

Just between you and me, isn't internal monologue the same thing as hearing voices? Like those crickets you used to start this internal monologue. Were they literal or figurative? Did you hear them?

JIM
In a way.

BRAIN
But isn't that a sign of...you know?

JIM
Not in our class. People get all rapturous about such things. 'Oh, what a great internal monologue, Sue. Class, you could all learn a lot from Sue's internal monologue.'
Meanwhile, *my* internal monologist is a mime.

BRAIN
Don't let Marcel hear you say that. You know how sensitive he is. I'll get him for you.

Short pause.

MARCEL
Sorry, I was on break.

JIM
Marcel, is that you?

MARCEL
Talk to me.

JIM
Actually, I need *you* to talk to *me*. If I show up in my writing class without some kind of 'internal monologue', I'll be shamed and shunned.

103

Jim Prime

MARCEL
Sounds like a tough group.

JIM
There's one guy there—the teacher's pet, I call him. He'll have some elaborate interior monologue about computers or sex, or computers having sex. Anything to please teacher.

MARCEL
Okay, okay. First I have to get in the mood. Can you get some chamomile tea and put the *Best of the Eagles* on iTunes?

JIM
Sure.

> *Sounds of tea being made: kettle singing, water pouring, spoon clinking in mug.*
> *MUSIC UP: Desperado, then fade to background*

JIM
Okay, there's *Desperado* playing in the background and the tea is just right.

> *Pause.*

JIM
What was that, Marcel?

MARCEL
I didn't say anything. Your stomach's growling. I'm still pondering. I don't think you realize the enormity of the task you've given me.

JIM
Well, that's wrong, for starters.

Beyond the Passage

MARCEL
What do you mean?

JIM
Trust me: 'enormity' doesn't mean what you think it means. I've been called on it twice now by teacher.

MARCEL
Awesomeness, then. Does that work?

JIM
Apparently.

MARCEL
Listen, Jimbo, you've gotta give me a little guidance. What are you writing about, anyway?

JIM
Well, it's a novel about a right whale that gets beached on Long Island that may or may not have been used to smuggle drugs from the Caribbean. And a fisherman named Josh who loves a girl named Holly who's visiting the island on summer vacation. Over the course of the summer they fall in love and have sex. Just once. She's sixteen and he's seventeen. She gets pregnant but he doesn't know that.

She disappears and he never sees her again, although he thinks about her often. Twenty years pass. His child, a daughter named Sophie, who is now a graduate student in marine biology at Acadia, comes to the island to help perform a necropsy on the dead whale.

She meets Josh, who kind of takes her under his wing, in a fatherly way. During a phone call home to her mother in Boston, Sophie happens to mention Josh.

Holly is now a recently-widowed photo-journalist. She hears the name of her long-ago summer fling, panics, and catches the next flight to Halifax. She rents a car and drives to the island. She's

105

Jim Prime

afraid that Sophie and Josh might figure out that they are, in fact, father-daughter. She doesn't know what to do.

BRAIN
Holy shit!

JIM
Exactly.

MARCEL
You're going to have a whale smuggling drugs?!

JIM
Okay, okay, it's a terrible idea! Everyone in class has told me so—and now you. I'll change it!

BRAIN
Relax, man.

JIM
Sorry, it's this writers' group. The pressure to perform has changed me.

MARCEL
Sounds horrible. So this Josh guy, he's still got the hots for Holly?

JIM
Crudely put, but yes.

MARCEL
And his daughter, what's her name again?

BRAIN
Sophie.

MARCEL

Beyond the Passage

Sophie doesn't suspect that Josh is her father?
JIM
Nope. There is some subtle foreshadowing of it, but she has no reason to connect the dots. Her mom, that's Holly, is about to tell her. That's where you come in.

MARCEL
You need me to come up with Holly's internal monologue before she informs her daughter, Sophie, that Josh is her father.

JIM
You've got it.

MARCEL
I'm an internal monologist, not a ventriloquist!

JIM
Sorry, I know it isn't easy.

MARCEL
Okay, okay. How about this? Write this down...

    Clears throat.

MARCEL
Holly stood on the high plateau of land that overlooked the entrance to Grand Passage. A slight onshore breeze ruffled her long auburn hair. She closed her eyes and breathed in the salt air, waiting for her daughter to arrive.
Why is this so hard? I'm a 38-year-old professional. Maybe I should just say it: 'Josh is your dad.'

No, sorry, Jimbo, that's not it. Too abrupt. Maybe...

'Soph, I have something that I need to tell you and I'm hoping that once you get past the initial shock, you'll understand and

Jim Prime

> know that nothing has really changed. Sophie...Josh is your father.'

No, too derivative of *Star Wars*. Maybe a bit more subtle, like,

> Things were different back then, Sophie. Having a baby before you were married was pretty scandalous.'

No, too long, too rehearsed.

> Will she ever trust me again? And what happens once I've told her? Do I stop there and let it sink in, or do I plunge ahead and tell her everything? Do I pull the band-aid off in one quick motion or do it more gradually?

And that, Jimbo, is how you write an internal monologue. You are welcome.

BRAIN
Wow...

JIM
Not bad, Marcel. I'll tweak it.

MARCEL
Tweak it?! It's perfect! Listen, pal, you try throwing your voice into a third party of the opposing sex, someone you hardly know. Out of the blue, just like that.

Let me give you a little insight into the life of an internal monologist. Day after day, week after week, you're called on to perform the most mundane, mind-numbing, artless tasks. Whatever you see or feel, I'm expected to comment on it. It's my job to say things that you can't or won't or shouldn't say out loud.

Like, for example, you were at the Valley Regional Hospital this morning waiting to give blood, right? Here are some nuggets from your internal monologue for that time. Before you thought to con-

108

sult with *moi*.

I took notes.

> *God, I wonder what's wrong with* that *guy? He looks terrible. Please don't sit next to me, fella.*
>
> *Geez, I'm number 115 and they just called number 4. What the hell am I paying taxes for?*
>
> *Hey, why is she cutting in line? She just arrived. Diabetic? So what? That's discrimination.*
>
> *Now there's something I can never un-see. Lose the stretchy pants, ma'am. You're not twenty anymore.*
>
> *Urology Department, 2nd Floor. Does that include proctologists? Don't think I ever met a proctologist, but then, how would I know?*
>
> *Hell-o! Who's this? Very nice indeed. Wait. Is she my daughter's age? Is it still wrong to notice a woman who's your daughter's age if your daughter is 36? I mean, there has to be a time limit on that. God, my pants are tight, they're cutting off circulation to my...I need to lose fifteen pounds, maybe twenty.*
>
> *Do I have $3.00 to get out of the parking lot?*

BRAIN
Oh. My. Gawd.

JIM
Is that me?

MARCEL
Not exactly 'To be or not to be', is it?

JIM
I see what you mean.

MARCEL

Jim Prime

So you're asking me to go from that disconnected drivel to something poignant, cogent, and meaningful, something that will move the plot forward, and you want me to do it in the voice of a complete stranger. And a woman, a species about which you know shockingly little for a man your age, I might add. And then you dare criticize me?!

JIM
You're right. Thank you. You did a good job.

MARCEL
Plus, your reading voice is terrible, like a strangulated seagull. It kills me having to put my beautiful words into that mouth. It's like Gilbert Gottfried reading the Gettysburg Address.

BRAIN
He has a point.

JIM
I said I'm sorry. Excellent work.

MARCEL
This isn't going to be a weekly thing, is it?

JIM
Naw, they'll be onto something new next week. Dialogue, maybe, or past pluperfect subjunctive. But I may need to call on you every so often.

MARCEL
Can I at least use 'enormity' when I talk to you?

JIM
Sure. I'll catch it in the edit.

MARCEL

Awesome!

Blackout

Jim Prime

The deer and the hunters

Luke clung to his father's leg as the men stood around the carcass of the large buck. The flickering light from two kerosene lamps penetrated the hay dust, bathing the drafty barn in diffused amber.

Except for his father, all the men were smoking. They passed barely-audible comments and the shadows cast by the lanterns gave their weathered faces a gaunt, hungry look.

Luke watched as they bound the deer's hind legs together with heavy twine. They threw a rope with an iron hook at one end over a beam and attached it to the twine.

His father and two of the men grabbed the free end of the rope and heaved until the deer was hanging free of the hay-strewn floor. Its eyes were open, its tongue lolling obscenely from its mouth.

His father expertly tied the rope off on a rusty floor ring.

Luke shuddered in the drafty barn and immediately hoped that no one had noticed. He glanced around and saw Carl Wilton grinning at him, showing rows of uneven yellow teeth.

"Whattaya think, boy?" Carl nudged the man next to him. "Feelin' a little queasy?"

The men laughed and Luke noticed that his father joined in. He gave a quick shake of his head and looked away, focusing hard on the deer.

A neighbour wearing yellow rain gear stepped forward, brandishing a long Bowie-style knife. He cut a hole under the deer's neck and then ran the knife upward through its underbelly to the hind end. The entrails spilled out and fouled the yellow hay with blood and offal.

Luke's eyes were now closed and remained shut until he heard his father say. "Good job, Hugh. Appreciate it. I'll bring over a few steaks."

The man nodded and left the barn. Luke could hear him turn on the water hose at the side of the barn to clean himself.

The men talked a while longer and then drifted away, leaving just Luke and his father.

"Well, what did you think of that, Luke?"

"I don't know."

"It's kind of scary the first time. I remember watching the first time my father cleaned a deer. But you'll get over it. It's all part of living in the country." He mussed his son's hair.

"Dad."

"Yeah?"

"I closed my eyes some of the time."

"So did I, the first time."

"Do I have to shoot deer when I grow up?"

"Well, no, not if you don't want to. Of course not."

"I don't think I'll want to."

"That's fine, Luke. I know it was kind of bloody."

"It wasn't just the blood, not mainly, anyway."

"Oh."

"It was the way the men laughed. That bothered me the most."

"Ah."

"You laughed too, dad."

"Yes, I did."

"Why?"

"I guess because Wilton expected it."

"But you don't like Wilton. I've heard you tell mom."

His father smiled. "Well, between you and me: no, I don't like him much."

"Then why did you laugh?"

His father paused and looked at his son. "Sometimes you do things when you're in a crowd that you wouldn't ordinarily do. I'm sorry I did."

"Yeah. Sometimes you have to, I guess."

Jim Prime

No second chances at first pitches

In the 1960s, Island schools had no sports teams to cheer for. After school we played full-contact soccer, in which body checking was not only tolerated, but encouraged. We played some pond hockey in winter, although the constant wind and salt air made for hubbly and treacherous ice.

For the most part, we saved our hero-worship for certain young drivers who used the serpentine ten-mile stretch of Long Island as their own person race track. Some of these speedsters became local legends: their exploits earned them the admiration of the male population and the attentions of all the pretty girls.

But summer was different. Summer was nonstop baseball, played on a field so rough that it would have made Neil Armstrong nostalgic for the surface of the moon. Discarded fish nets served as backstops, fog added another dimension to pursuing fly balls, and cows grazed in the outfield, oblivious to the action. Their presence presented an obvious distraction and specific ground rules had to be drawn up for balls that landed in cow pies. The home-run fence was barbed wire and was electrified.

Somehow none of this hampered our enjoyment of the games, and the location of the field on an elevated plateau of more-or-less level pastureland afforded a breathtaking view of both the Bay of Fundy down the right field line and St. Mary's Bay a few miles beyond third base. This was heaven, I used think. No place in the world like this.

One of the countless perks of growing up on Long Island was that you could pick up Boston radio stations, day or night. The only time my transistor dial strayed from WMEX was when I tuned in to Red Sox games. Listening to Curt Gowdy and Ned Martin do the

Beyond the Passage

play-by-play for those games was captivating and their descriptions of Fenway Park sparked my imagination like nothing I had ever heard. Terms like "the Monster," the "triangle," and Pesky's Pole all sounded so exotic and the background sound of vendors yelling their two syllable "Be-ah"—that's beer—and, even better, "Be-ah, he-ah!" was like a siren call.

I answered that call years later and it was everything I had expected it to be, and more.

July 5, 2011. Nova Scotia Day at Fenway Park. As one of the founding member of the Bluenose Bosox Brotherhood, I was one of well over 250 NS fans who journeyed south for the game between the Red Sox and the visiting Toronto Blue Jays.

Nova Scotia baseball fans had made this southern migration for generations, back to the days when Babe Ruth was better known as a Red Sox pitching ace than for the hitting prowess that would make him a legend with the NY Yankees. They went to watch Ruth and Williams and Yaz and Big Papi and a host of others. Because for Maritimers the Boston Red Sox were the home team.

Later, the Montreal Expos and then Toronto Blue Jays came along to dilute the fandom pool, but a core of diehard Bosox fans remained, defiant and oblivious to any patriotic attachment to the Canadian upstarts. I was one of those diehard fans.

I'd learned that I'd be the 'First Pitch Guy' less than five hours earlier. Other candidates included notable Nova Scotians such as singer Anne Murray, actress Ellen Page and Boston Bruin Brad Marchand. Marchand was the obvious choice. Only weeks earlier he had helped lead the Boston Bruins to their first Stanley Cup championship since 1972. Rumour had it that he might even bring the Cup to the ballpark for an encore visit.

Other contenders included a Canadian military veteran, a long-time fan who once held Red Sox season tickets despite having to commute to games from NS; hockey great Sidney Crosby, and Bill "Spaceman" Lee, who played ball briefly in NS after his Major League career was over.

I knew that my colleagues had thrown my name into the mix, but I didn't like my chances, so when a Red Sox official told me it

Jim Prime

would indeed be me, I received the news with a combination of shock and awe. (I should make it perfectly clear that I was not chosen *instead* of the various luminaries mentioned above. The truth is that none of them were available to, or even reachable by, the BBB. So there I was, waiting at the bottom of the barrel when they reached it.)

Although outwardly calm, I immediately felt a huge responsibility. Not only was I representing our province and country, but I was also thinking of Fenway Park itself. I didn't want to let the old girl down.

And so it was that, at the age of 62 years, eleven months, I was about to ascend the mound at Fenway Park for the first and last time in my life. As we waited for the ceremony to begin, the Red Sox ambassador asked if I wanted to throw from in front of the mound or on the mound. Without hesitation I said, "Oh, definitely from the mound."

That was a mistake.

Hotel parking lots don't have mounds, and that is where I'd done my warm-up two days earlier on the slim chance that I might be selected. It was a fifteen-minute workout for the sole purpose of confirming that I could actually propel the ball 60 feet 6 inches in a more or less straight line. I succeeded in that goal and declared myself fit for action.

But that was the asphalt at the Portland, Maine Econo Lodge and this was the mound at Fenway Park. Nevertheless, my arm felt good and I was satisfied that, if the call came, I was ready.

The Red Sox staff was supportive, encouraging, practised at putting people at ease. The ambassador was a pert young lady with a winning smile and an easy self-assurance that suggested she had done this before. She introduced me to my catcher, an athletic woman with her long blond hair in a ponytail. She also had done this countless times. For me it was the first.

I remembered something that Jerry Remy had said on a recent broadcast: *just get the ball and throw it. Don't try to put on a show, not unless you're Dennis Eckersley or Will Farrell.*

116

Beyond the Passage

When I was selected, my fellow travellers had asked me what I'd be throwing. The knuckler? The curve? The slider? Joining in the joke, I just smiled and said I thought I'd bring the heat.

They led us to a staging area somewhere in the bowels of Fenway, and gave us our briefing. Present were the honour guard, the people assigned to hold the NS flag and a banner, the honorary bat boys, the singer of the national anthems and the winner of a Red Cross award. This was a big, big deal, I realized. Bigger than even I had imagined.

It's truly amazing how many things can pass through the human mind on a trip to the mound at Fenway Park. I was wearing a Red Sox jersey, shirttails out, with the number 9 on the back and my last name in capital letters above it. As a Governor of Red Sox Nation for NS, the first such designation outside of the United States, I had been presented with the jersey earlier that same day. I had requested the number because I was a lifelong fan of the Splendid Splinter.

Only now was I struck by the significance of wearing the iconic digit onto the field. Who did I think I was? Surely not Ted Williams. Ted was the greatest hitter in the history of the game and the greatest Red Sox player of all time. I felt like a marked man, the scarlet number there for all to see.

Number 9 came with great expectations attached. I wanted to remove it and replace it with something more fitting to my station, perhaps one of those high spring training numbers, like 72 or 85. Or perhaps a 0—or one of those 1/2s you used to see sported by baseball clowns in the Forties.

My one consolation was that Ted was known for hitting the ball, not throwing it. I wondered if he had also felt like an imposter on his lone Major League pitching stint on August 24, 1940. He had allowed three hits and one run in two innings while mopping up in a 12-1 loss to Detroit. But he had also struck out slugger Rudy York. All I had to do was get the ball somewhere near home plate.

A rush of such thoughts assaulted me on the lonely trek to the mound, and images that were at once real and surreal filled my senses. Straight ahead of me stood the Wall. Even from the deepest

117

Jim Prime

recesses of the stands you knew it was close, but now it looked as intimate as a backyard fence. The grass was somehow greener than I thought it would be, the chalk lines whiter, the dirt much redder.

I had been told not to step on the baseline, so I jumped it, thinking of all the superstitious ballplayers who had done the same thing for different reasons.

I looked around. Fans were still filing into the ballpark and settling into their seats. I spotted my name in the left field lights and pointed it out to my catcher, who smiled tolerantly.

I turned around and saw that I was looking back at myself from the giant scoreboard screen. The CEREMONIAL FIRST PITCH, JIM PRIME, NOVA SCOTIA. Behind second base, the colour guard of Nova Scotian firemen were displaying the Canadian and American flags while two others held the historic Nova Scotia standard.

I reached the mound and settled into a spot just short of the rubber. I had received strict instructions not to touch the game ball, which was sitting in pristine whiteness behind the rubber. I was also instructed not to touch the resin bag which lay beside it. These two items were sacrosanct and to defile them was akin to sacrilege.

Before the ceremony, a friend had taken me aside and counselled me to enjoy the moment, to look around and drink it all in. The trouble was that I was already drunk with the enormity of the moment. My mind wasn't so much drinking it in, it was swimming in it. I was already aware that I was standing in a place where Babe Ruth had once toed the rubber, where Mel Parnell and Bill Lee and Lefty Grove and Jim Lonborg and Roger Clemens and Pedro Martinez and Curt Schilling had worked under pressure that made my meaningless toss to home plate insignificant. This was where Dick Radatz had repeatedly killed the Yankees. Where Luis Tiant had pitched as if conducting a symphony orchestra. Where current stars with names like Papelbon and Bard and Beckett and Wakefield twirled their magic.

I did glance around, albeit nervously, and a kind of calm came over me, possibly like that experienced in the eye of a hurricane.

Beyond the Passage

I had actually played a lot of baseball in my earlier days and, while I was never a good hitter, I fancied myself as a pretty fair defensive first baseman, with an arm more than lively enough for infield duties. It was a good, if not strong arm.

But my baseball experience came on a small island in the Bay of Fundy with only the seagulls as spectators and a patched herring net as our backstop. Games sometimes had to be called on account of the fog which crept across our field and swallowed outfielders up like the corn fields in *Field of Dreams*.

There was no fog at Fenway, except for the personal one that had started to envelop me. It wasn't fear that I felt, more a foreboding.

Off to my left I was vaguely aware of the Red Sox dugout, with players milling about. Luckily, players don't watch fans throw baseballs. It goes against the natural order of things. Later, photographs confirmed that only manager Terry Francona was actually watching—but he seemed to be watching intently. My surmise is that he was looking for pitching help, an ineffective John Lackey having frittered away the previous night's game.

To my right was the Blue Jays' dugout, with the team that supposedly represents my homeland. Were they pulling for this traitorous Red Sox fan to fail? Straight ahead and way up was the Press Box, filled with Boston writers famed for their wit, cynicism and venom. *If they found reason to criticize Ted and Yaz, what would they do to me?* I thought.

Once more I felt like an outsider, a fraud, an imposter. But I also knew that this was something that every Red Sox fan dreams of: standing on the mound at Fenway Park, the epicentre of our baseball world.

In case you are ever given the chance that I was, please remember. THERE IS NO WARM-UP FOR THROWING OUT A FIRST PITCH. I may make it my epitaph. The pert girl hands you the ball and a voice from above, public address announcer Carl Beane, says, "Alright Jim, let's see that pitch."

Perhaps it was the height of the mound. Perhaps it was the enormity of the moment. Perhaps it was simply that my body was

Jim Prime

no longer a baseball body' it was now a baseball-watching body.

As soon as the ball left my hand I knew that it was wide to the right. Not wide as in a brush back pitch to Dewey Evans, but wide as in *Watch out, bat boys!* wide. I'm a mature adult but at that moment I fervently wished that I could somehow stop that ball in midair and have it return to my hand for a second chance.

But there are no second chances where first pitches are concerned, only second guessing.

My catcher, the pretty, athletic blonde, made a valiant attempt to get it, but even Carlton Fisk couldn't have cornered this one. I turned away in disgust, grasped my head with both hands and no doubt swore loudly.

I recovered quickly as the catcher arrived, handed me the traitorous ball and smiled warmly. It was over.

There were no boos—at least, I don't hear any. The truth is that, unless the first pitch is thrown by family, friend or a celebrity, most people could care less. My friend Dave Ritcey, who was on the field holding a Nova Scotia banner, later claimed he booed, but you can hear nothing in a vacuum—and I heard nothing.

If the walk to the mound had been exciting and hopeful, the walk from the mound was that of a condemned man. Condemned to relive that moment over and over.

It's hard to express how disappointed I was in myself. As I left the field, I felt the eyes of Fenway on me. I wished that the fog that I had played in back on Long Island would sweep in and envelop me in its embrace. I avoided eye contact all the way up the aisle next to the Red Sox dugout.

Near the top of the first section of seats, an elderly man stuck out his hand and said, 'Good job.' I could scarcely make eye contract with this most gracious of men as I voiced a terse. 'Thanks.'

For the first few days, I prayed that time could reverse itself and I could have just one more go. I often caught myself talking to myself out loud, even with others present. I'd wake up thinking that it hadn't happened yet, that I had another chance.

Photographic evidence of the aftermath of my chuck was deleted and/or removed from my home and a small ransom has been

Beyond the Passage

offered for the return of originals. When people ask me how I did, I tell them that I killed four nuns in the fifth row.

But you know, those people still look at me with envy. They say that the quality of the throw doesn't matter. The important thing is that I did something that most people will never have a chance to do.

In retrospect I look back on the event with a mixture of pride and embarrassment—a bittersweet moment, by the very definition of the word. I no longer have night sweats, and the flashbacks have all but disappeared. In fact, the shame I felt has turned into a kind of pride. Not in the throw itself, but in the fact that I did it.

I have three pictures that I will always treasure. One is of me in the set position. One is of my windup, and one is just after I released the ball. They all look pretty good. Like I knew what I was doing. I also have the ball, complete with sacred Fenway Park dirt on it.

My grandchildren will hear tales of my only on-field appearance at Fenway Park. They will hear colourful details of my march to the mound, kicking the rubber and unleashing the pitch. The details will be highly colourful and highly inaccurate.

Jim Prime

The Phantom of Fenway

> *Boston Herald*, April 20, 1912
> Obituary -
> Phineas E. Strunk, 30, died suddenly on April 20, at
> 2:30 pm as the result of a freak automobile accident
> near the new baseball park known as Fenway. He
> leaves behind a wife, Doris, and two children, John
> and Mary. A lifelong Red Sox fan, he also enjoyed
> playing in an amateur league in his hometown of
> Lynn. Funeral arrangements are pending.

My name is Phineas E. Strunk, deceased. As you can see, I wasn't always a ghost. I started out as a pretty normal guy. Wonderful wife, two great kids, nice house in Lynn only about ten blocks from the coast, and a two-year-old Ford Runabout with just two payments left. I drove a newspaper delivery truck for the *Boston Post*, which is also deceased, as is each of the dozen or so dailies that used to keep the city and its satellite cities informed.

I wasn't an editor or writer or anything like that (although that was my goal). That's why I've hired a ghost writer to tell my story. I was just a common labourer. I'd drop the stacks of papers off at newspaper stands and corner stores and places like that. I loved being in the news business.

One spring day I was driving my jalopy past the brand new Fenway Park. It was April 20th, 1912. In fact, it was the day they played the first-ever major league game there and I admit it wasn't part of my usual route. I drove by just to be able to say I was there. Wrong

122

Beyond the Passage

place, wrong time. Get this. A baseball flew out of the ball park and killed me.

Well okay, technically the ball didn't actually kill me. It hit the windshield and scared the bejeebers out of me. I swerved and hit a brick wall. No wonder they called it the dead ball era! That's a laugh. Yeah, I died laughing.

I found out later that it happened in batting practice when the guys were fooling around. Apparently someone bet Hugh Bradley, the Red Sox first baseman, that he couldn't hit a ball over the left field wall. Well, apparently he could.

I've got no beef with him though. A few days later, on April 26, he hit the very first homer at Fenway (it was over the left field wall, too) and I was there to cheer him on, no baloney.

One birth (Fenway) and one death (mine).

The incident didn't get much attention in the Boston papers. I guess the Titanic hitting an iceberg was more dramatic than me hitting a brick wall. That was the front page news, I do remember that—it even pushed aside the opening of Fenway.

Anyway, there I was, dead, right outside spanking-new Fenway Park.

Those early years from 1912-1918 were halcyon days. I was freshly dead—and loving it! The Red Sox were winning. Since they opened their doors in 1912 to a winning season, they had won again in 1915, 1916 and 1918. That was four World Series championships in seven years at the new Fenway! (Plus one that they won in the old Huntington Grounds).

I was on top of the world. I thought of myself as their good luck charm—kind of a guardian angel.

Since I had died right out front, it was decreed by The Ultimate Ump, as I call him, that I spend the rest of eternity here at Fenway. They have very specific rules about these sorts of things up there. If you die at a sausage factory then you haunt the sausage factory. If you bite the dust at the post office, you'll be the post office ghost. To give you a recent example from the literature of the day, Hogwarts ghosts remain at Hogwarts.

Jim Prime

The rule of thumb is that you haunt the building nearest where you 'bought the farm,' unless it's under 1000 square feet, in which case you can choose another building within a five-mile radius. They're pretty fair about that—wouldn't leave you at a road side or in a gas station toilet or something. Very fair, indeed.

Of course, I'd like to be able to go to Florida for spring training with the guys, but when I suggested it, they said, "Phin, it ain't gonna happen. Against the rules." Just like that. End of discussion.

I felt at home at Fenway from that very first day. It was called Fenway because it was built on the Fens, a low, marshy area of the city that had never been developed. But inside those gates, the park was beautiful, lush green field with lots of nooks and crannies to explore.

There are other Ground Rules, or Firmament Rules, as they call them, for ballpark ghosts (you probably thought I was the only one, but Wrigley in Chicago has a guy and so did the old Yankee Stadium). The # 1 rule (rule 46(c)) states that you can't affect the outcome of the game.

You've heard of the Golden Rule. Well, this Diamond Rule is just as binding: "No ghost shall alter the outcome of a baseball game or influence mortals to do so."

I've followed that Diamond Rule pretty closely, too, with a few small lapses. Darn few when you think it's been more than a century! Sometimes I just get caught up in the excitement and things happen.

Fortunately, they are a pretty forgiving lot up there at Head Office. They're famous for it, really. I'm not like that angel Clarence in *It's a Wonderful Life*, who had to earn his wings. They know I ain't perfect.

Hard to believe it's been 100 years. I mean, 100 years!! I'm as old as Fenway Park. 130 years if you count my physical life, but we're not really supposed to do that. Clean slate and all that.

Fenway was so shiny and new, and so big! I remember the bright red brick on the façade and the excitement of the crowd on that opening day. The smell of popcorn and hot dogs and newly-mown grass. I was a bit distracted, having just died and all, but some

124

Beyond the Passage

things you just never forget.

During my mortal years, I guess I was a pretty nice guy, always offered a helping hand. I fully expected to go to Heaven, and I guess in a way I did. Fenway is certainly heavenly, especially for a Red Sox fan like me. I could have gone to the other place, by which I mean Yankee Stadium.

Fenway's not the real thing, of course. Heaven has a much larger capacity and their version of the left field wall is really more of a pearly gate. But who's complaining? All in all, I've had a good, full death.

Technically I'm a ghost, but some people would call me an apparition, a poltergeist, or spirit. I'm not ectoplasm, and please don't call me that.

Personally, I prefer phantom because I'm a fan and I'm also a ghost. Get it? The Phantom of Fenway, that's me. It has a nice ring to it, doesn't it? Like fandom.

My wife and kids took my demise pretty hard, of course. They couldn't even come to games for the longest time. But life goes on, and they eventually started to live normal lives. My wife got remarried to a Sox fan and my kids grew up and got jobs. I saw them and the grandkids and great grandkids at the park over the years. It was always nice.

So that's it—I'm the Fenway Park ghost. A lot of people think that Babe Ruth haunts the place. They think that the so-called "curse of the Bambino", supposedly responsible for an 86-year drought in World Series championships, meant that Babe has been hanging around the place since he was shipped off to the Yankees in 1918. Like some malevolent presence. Members of the cleaning crew claim that they hear him taking batting practice.

Nonsense of course. Believe me, if the Babe was at Fenway, he'd be at the beer stand, not taking batting practice. He's somewhere in New York, probably haunting a tavern.

There are certain stereotypes about ghosts that I need to address. We don't say "Boo!" Ridiculous. I will admit that "Boo" Ferriss was my favorite player when he played here, but that was just coincidence. The only time I really say boo is when the Yankees are

125

Jim Prime

in town, and even then it's drowned out by all of the other booing, not to mention profanities that would have condemned me straight to Hell; i.e., Yankee Stadium.

Then there's the misconception that we're evil and that's why we've been condemned to an eternity of haunting. Not true. There are bad ghosts, no doubt, but I'm not one.

You see, the Ultimate Ump loves baseball. Loves it! The first four words in the Bible are 'In the big inning,' although an unfortunate misprint has mislead many people.

The Fenway assignment was a reward for my loyalty to the Red Sox. I can see why some would consider it a punishment—even a damnation—given the team's history, but I'm a pretty upbeat kind of guy, and in the context of immortality, what difference does a century of losing matter? Life goes on...well, you know what I mean.

It can get kind of lonely when the Red Sox are on the road. But sometimes there are concerts. Neil Diamond played here and so did the Beatles and Rolling Stones. I saw Keith Richards and I thought to myself, *He looks like death warmed over*. I'm still waiting for the Grateful Dead to show up.

Winters are the worst. Not that I get cold or anything. I mean, I can hardly catch my death of cold, can I? Ha! That cracks up my buddy Neville, the Museum ghost, every time I tell it. But there's nothing much to do in the off-season. I joined in a few guided tours of the ballpark and last year there was even a Bruins game here! But the summers are really my thing.

As I said, I got the job at the *Post*, hoping to get my foot in the door and eventually become a sports writer. I met a few of the editors and finally got to write a couple of player profiles. Now I'm a ghost writer. I write for the *Celestial Times* and, believe me, there is no fake news in that paper. 100% accurate 100% of the time. Makes the gossip columns kind of boring, though.

Who is writing this piece? You may well ask. I contacted Jim Prime, and discovered that he believes in ghosts. Of course, he also believes in Sasquatches, UFOs, gremlins, and zombies that run amok destroying small towns. But since Sox fan Stephen King

Beyond the Passage

didn't respond to my ads, it was Jim or no one.

I dare say I am the biggest expert on the Red Sox living or dead. Problem is, I have no one to share my knowledge with. Oh sure, I have ghost friends. There's Nev from the Museum of Fine Arts and Peg from the Mary Baker Eddy Library and Mr. and Mrs. O'Reilly from the Gardner Museum, and Mario, a violinist from the Berklee College of Music, and so on. Nice folks, but not necessarily big baseball fans. We meet at Dunkin Donuts in the Concourse to smell the coffee every now and again and they humour me, but they're more into the cultural scene.

When I talk to them about our problem at first base, they think I'm talking about an orchestra, for cryin' out loud. That's when I tell my "It was the bottom of the ninth and the bassists were loaded" joke. But they still don't get it.

I ought to write a book about Fenway. I think I am highly qualified, and there's a lot I want to say. I've seen every Red Sox game from April 1912 to today. Every one! Regular season, All-Star games, playoffs and World Series. I have been in every nook and cranny of the ballpark. I have watched games from the press box, from inside the Green Monster, from Ted's Red Seat in the right field bleachers, from the top of both foul poles and the flag pole, from the pitcher's mound, the on-deck circle, and both dugouts. I've seen the first homer, the 10,000[th] homer, the first Red Sox no-hitter and the next eight, the first night game, the longest game (9/3/1981—Jerry Remy had six hits), two unassisted triple plays, and the longest home run ever hit at Fenway. I've overheard conversations on the mound, in the bullpen and in the dressing room. I've seen Speaker and Hooper, and Ruth and Foxx and Williams and Yaz and Jimmie, and Nomar and Manny and Papi and Pedroia and Boegarts.

Even though I've never caught a foul ball (part of that disembodied thing I was talking about), I've had several pass through me and that made me mad. I know I coulda caught them. I mean, I'm not Dick Stuart, who was so bad at first base that they called him Dr. Strangeglove. I've seen the Red Sox at their best, and I've endured 86 years without a World Series championship.

Jim Prime

In short, I have seen it all and heard it all. I am the ultimate fan —the Phantom of Fenway.

Earlier I mentioned the 'Ground Rules', the Diamond Rule being the most important. I'll repeat it in case you weren't paying attention. 'No ghost shall alter the outcome of a baseball game or influence mortals to do so. Interference of this sort will result in your being banned (in my case, banished) from Fenway Park.'

In 1975, in the eleventh inning of the sixth game of the World Series against Cincinnati, I came close to breaking that 11th commandment. Carlton Fisk was at the plate and he hit a long, high drive to left field. It was curving foul and looked like it would be just another long strike. I considered changing the path of that ball, I really did. I thought long and hard about it: we can do that sort of thing in a split second.

I resisted and the ball hit the foul pole and stayed fair and the Red Sox won and it remains one of the greatest moments in Fenway history. I was proud of myself for not intervening.

Then one day I was talking to the Big Guy. He'd had a few ambrosias and was talking a blue streak. Suddenly he comes out with it. "Remember Fisk's homer," he said.

"Of course," I replied.

"I did that," he said, very sheepishly. Can you imagine the Big Guy sounding sheepish?

The next day He denied that He'd ever said it. In 2004, or as I call it 86 AD (Annual Doom), I decided to be proactive and follow the precedent He'd set. It started pretty innocently. Most of my on-field moves were small. I turned a few sure outs into base hits for our side.

The most important thing I did was to instill the spirit of the game in every player as they entered the ballpark. In fact, the only blatant offence that I committed was in the American League Championship Series against the New York Yankees in 2004. I confess that I did intervene—big time. I mean, we had come so far. I didn't want it to end.

We lost the first game 10-7 and I did nothing. We lost game two 3-1 and I just sat on my hands. We lost the third game 19-8! A hu-

Beyond the Passage

miliating disaster and I still did nothing. We were on the brink of elimination. That's when I asked for an audience with the Big Guy.

After a brief chat about the weather, I very timidly asked him if I could do something about the World Series. He paused and said, and I'll never forget His words, "What did you have in mind? Whatever, it is has to be subtle."

I told Him my plans and He just nodded but I could tell he was intrigued, even pleased. As I thanked Him and turned to leave His presence, He spoke again. It's amazing how much his voice sounds like Ted Williams, it really is.

Anyway, He said...let's say He intoned, or quothed: "I'm only doing this to even things out, you know. There are Dark Forces at work in aid of the Evil Empire."

I knew what he meant by 'Evil Empire'.

Well, the rest is history. We won game four in dramatic fashion. With the Yankees leading 4-3 in the bottom of the ninth, pinch runner Dave Roberts was on first and everyone in the ballpark and millions watching on TV knew he was going to try to steal second. And he did steal second, on a play that was so close that the human eye could not distinguish safe from out. He was safe.

That's it. That's all I did. I gave him what's called the benefit of the doubt. Roberts scored on a single by Bill Mueller to tie the game. The Sox won in the bottom of 12th on a two-run homer by Big Papi Ortiz. Final score 6-4.

It's a sin to steal so I guess you could say that Roberts and I both erred on that play.

Miraculously we won games five and six and by the time we reached game seven, the Yankees were finished.

Funny thing is, I only intervened in that fourth game. All the boys needed was a bit of a lift. They did the rest all on their own.

Then they met the St. Louis Cardinals in the World Series. The last two times these teams met in the Fall Classic were in 1946 and 1967, and both times the Cards broke our hearts. This time, the Sox rolled over them, winning in four straight games.

After 86 years we were finally world champions. I know that in relation to eternity—which is how things are measured on my side

Jim Prime

of death—86 years isn't much, but that whole "Wait'll next year" thing was getting kind of old.

Since then we've won four World Series in this century and I can honestly say I've maintained my hands-off policy, although I can't speak for others—or the Big Guy, for that matter.

It's a great game, baseball. The only game with no time limit, you know. Much like eternity.

Beyond the Passage

The magic baseball card

Playing baseball on an island in the Bay of Fundy presents special challenges. For one thing, there's the fog. It creeps slowly in from the bay and moves across the field, swallowing first the outfielders, then the second baseman and finally the pitcher and catcher.

Jeffrey Curtis hated playing baseball in the fog. He heard the crack of the bat, and was pretty sure that the ball was coming toward him in centre field, but he couldn't see it. Then, at the last split second, he flicked his glove upward toward a round white blur and grabbed it for the final out in the top of the ninth inning.

"We need radar out there," Jeffrey yelled to his friend Gary, as they jogged in for their turn at bat.

"Count your blessings," Gary shouted back. "At least the outfield is fairly level. The infield is so rough it makes the surface of the moon look like a putting green."

They both laughed.

The score was knotted at 3-3 and Jeffrey was first up at bat. Someone yelled, "All we need is one run, Jeff! Launch one for the Schooners!" He smiled to himself and patted his hip pocket to make sure his good luck piece was still there. It was only a bubble-gum card—a laminated rectangle of cardboard with a picture of a baseball player on one side and the player's statistics on the other. But this was no ordinary card. This was a 1956 Ted Williams, that his grandfather gave to him just a few weeks before the old man had died. "It'll bring you luck," he had said, tousling Jeffrey's hair fondly. "And remind you to be patient and get a good ball to hit— just like Ted did."

Jeffrey and his grandfather had spent many long hours together fishing for brook trout and talking about baseball—today's base-

Jim Prime

ball and the baseball of bygone days. They disagreed about domed stadiums, artificial turf, and the Designated Hitter rule. But they agreed that Ted Williams had been the greatest hitter of all time.

His grandfather came to all of Jeffrey's games and cheered loudly, especially when his grandson came to the plate. This was the first game of the season and the first without his grandfather there to watch him.

Jeffrey felt powerful with the bat in his hand and the card in his pocket. As he stepped into the batters' box, he tried to remember the advice that his grandfather had given him. "Remember Ted's golden rules for hitting. Get a good ball to hit. Proper thinking at the plate. Be quick."

He squinted through the mist at the Westport Whitecaps' pitcher, 60' 6" away, and cocked his bat.

The first pitch was waist-high and on the inside corner. He jumped on it, driving it deep into right field. As he rounded first base, he could barely make out the ball dropping beyond the out-fielder's outstretched glove. Between second and third he made up his mind to try to beat the throw to the plate. The Whitecaps' second baseman took the relay and fired homeward, but Jeffrey slid in under the catcher's tag for the winning run. Final score: Freeport Schooners 4, Westport Whitecaps 3.

His teammates surrounded him, clapping him on the back. Out of habit, he glanced around to where his grampie usually sat at the end of the bench, but there was only an empty space.

It was Saturday afternoon and when Jeffrey got home after the game, he could see that something was up. His father and mother and sister Catherine were sitting at the kitchen table with maps and brochures spread out in front of them.

His father looked up and smiled. "What was the score?"

"Four-three for the good guys," Jeffrey said, deciding not to brag about his game-winning hit. "What's going on here?"

Just then he noticed a glossy brochure with the words, *Things to Do in Boston,* on the front. His heart skipped a beat.

"We're planning our summer vacation," his dad said, still grinning.

Beyond the Passage

This could only mean one thing, and Jeffrey automatically felt for the Ted Williams card and tapped it three times for luck. The card never let him down before. *Please let it be a trip to Boston to see some ball games. Please!*

Catherine looked up from a list she was making. "I'm going to Boston with Mom, and you and dad are going fishing," she blurted excitedly.

Jeffrey looked from his sister to his father. This had to be a bad joke. But his dad was nodding his head.

"That's right, we're going salmon fishing on the Miramichi River in New Brunswick. What do you think of that?"

Jeffrey opened his mouth to speak but stopped abruptly. The news had been announced like a present, so he did his best to act pleased. But he wasn't. It was as if Ted Williams had struck out with two out and the bases loaded in the bottom of the ninth in the last at-bat in the seventh game of the World Series.

"Cath and I are staying with your aunt Molly," his mother said. "She hasn't been too well and needs a little help. She's going to be fine, though, and this will give us a chance to do some shopping, visit some art galleries."

"Are you going to a ballgame?" he asked sheepishly.

"Why, yes! Your uncle Herbert bought tickets for a couple of games."

Jeffrey's mind raced. *Catherine is going to be in Boston with Mom watching the Boston Red Sox play at Fenway Park. Meanwhile, I'll be up the creek with dad and the only bites I'll probably get will be from gigantic mosquitoes. And Cath isn't even a baseball fan!*

~

Three weeks later, Jeffrey was looking out the window of the log cabin his father had rented on the banks of the Miramichi River. It was 6:05 a.m. and the morning sun was already sending shafts of light through the pine trees.

His father was standing over a sizzling pan of bacon and eggs. He used a spatula to transfer the fry-up to two plates, added two

Jim Prime

slices of toast from the toaster, and put them on the table.

They sat across from each other and ate in silence for a minute until his father spoke. "Look, son. I know you'd rather have gone to Boston to see the Red Sox play. I promise that will happen someday. I just thought...well, I've been very busy with my work lately and I thought it would be nice for just the two of us to spend some time together. I loved fishing with my own dad and I always learned something new."

Jeff was surprised. He hadn't really thought about how often his dad had been away from home on business. Maybe because he'd always had Granddad. But more than that, he thought he'd been able to hide his feelings about not going to Boston.

"It's okay, dad," he said, forcing a smile. "We Red Sox fans are used to disappointments."

His father smiled. "I know you miss your grandfather. You two were always together. I miss him, too. He was my father, remember. Fishing is really my sport but you'll be happy to know that he also taught me a little about baseball. Did you know that Ted Williams hit a homer in his last time at bat?"

Of course Jeffrey knew. But he had no idea that his dad knew stuff like that.

His father continued, "Did you know he was the last ballplayer to hit .400 for a season?"

Jeffrey smiled patiently. "Dad, I don't want to hurt your feelings but I think I know just about everything there is to know about Ted Williams."

It was his father's turn to smile patiently. "Maybe so," he said, "We'll see. Before our week is over you might just learn something new about your hero."

By 7:15 they were at the river, casting for Atlantic salmon. Jeffrey was surprised to see the long smooth casts his father made. As they fished, they talked about baseball and every so often there would be another Ted Williams question.

"Did you know that he hit a homer every sixteen times at bat, on average? That he won two MVP awards and the Triple Crown twice? That he lost almost five years out of his career during war-

Beyond the Passage

time and still hit 521 homers?"

"Yes, dad I know all that," said Jeffrey. But even though he knew all the answers, it was great to have someone to talk baseball with again.

"Do you still have that card that your grandfather gave you?"

Jeffrey was a bit embarrassed. He didn't think anyone else knew about the card. "Yes. I've got it with me."

He reached into his pocket but when he pulled the card out it slipped through his wet fingers and dropped into the fast moving river. He made a grab for it, but couldn't move fast enough in his clumsy hip waders.

"Get it dad," he yelled, but it was too late. The plastic-coated card was bobbing wildly in the current.

"We've got to get it back!" he cried desperately.

"The river narrows just below here," his father said as they clambered toward the shore. "Maybe it'll snag on the rocks." He didn't sound very hopeful.

As they made their way around the river's bend, they saw a tall man with a fishing rod. He was bending down to scoop something from the water. He examined it closely and started to laugh.

Just then the man spotted Jeffrey and his father on the shore. "Is this thing yours?" he said, wading toward them and holding up the card.

There was a smile on his tanned face and somehow Jeffrey thought he looked familiar, like a long-ago friend who had gotten older.

"Yes, sir," he panted, taking the card. "Thank you." His voice was ragged with relief. "It slipped out of my hand. It's my good luck card. My grandfather gave it to me."

Jeffrey realized he was babbling and stopped abruptly.

"Is this guy your dad?" the tall man asked.

"Yes, sir." He waited for his father to introduce himself, but instead the two men shook hands like old friends.

"Then you must be Jeffrey, the ballplayer I've heard so much about."

Jeffrey was puzzled.

Jim Prime

"Maybe I'd better explain, son," his dad said. "This is...Ted Williams."

Jeffrey looked as if he'd seen a ghost. The man standing on the shore was Ted Williams. He looked at the likeness on the card and back at Ted Williams. "No wonder you looked so familiar," he stammered, "but..."

"I told you that you might learn something new this week," his dad said. "I guess you didn't know that Ted Williams has had a camp on this river since 1955."

"I sure didn't," Jeffrey said, beaming like a searchlight.

"That's how we met. I've fished with him a few times. I told him about you and he invited us to join him for dinner tonight at his lodge."

The rest of the day was like a dream. Jeffrey talked baseball with Ted Williams and listened as his dad and Williams discussed salmon flies and favourite salmon pools. Jeffrey told him all about his grandfather and how they fished together sometimes. He told him about his grandfather teaching him Ted's golden rules of hitting.

That night, tired but happy, the father and son made their way back to their own cabin. Jeffrey pulled the baseball card from his pocket and held it tightly in his palm. In one short day, he'd met his hero, Ted Williams, and discovered a new friend to talk baseball and fishing with, his dad.

The magic was still alive!

Beyond the Passage

Mary and Harry's Obituaries

Harry and Mary O'Leary are sitting in their sparse office, rehearsing a TV commercial.

"Okay, let's give it another try. Hi, I'm Mary," says Mary.

"And I'm Harry," Harry says.

"And this is Mary and Harry's Obituaries," they say in unison, looking directly into the computer camera.

Harry and Mary are owners of Harry and Mary's Obituaries, a start-up business located in a run-down strip mall on the outskirts of Dartmouth, Nova Scotia. They are making an ad for their new business.

Mary is seated casually on the edge of the desk and is speaking in a solemn, soothing voice. "Have you recently lost a loved one and want to give them a nice send-off?"

Harry, who is standing next to his wife, puts his hand on her shoulder. "But maybe writing wasn't your 'thing' in high school," he says. "That shouldn't prevent you from expressing your condolences to grieving family and friends. Remember, obituaries aren't just for the person being written about, they're for the living. The live audience, so to speak. Sure, an obituary says a lot about the dead, but it says a lot about *you*, the writer, too. Do you want people to think you don't care? Do you want your friends and neighbours to judge you because you can't pay proper tribute to a dear one who has gone to the Great Beyond? Even worse, do you want friends to think that you don't have the skills to put together such a tribute?"

Mary looks up at her husband and nods meaningfully. "So true, Harry," she says.

137

Jim Prime

Then she faces the camera again. "We at Mary and Harry's Obituaries are here to help. We have the perfect words and just the right phrases, adjectives, adverbs and verbs—mostly past tense, of course—to express what you feel at this sad time."

"Right you are, Mary," Harry says. He smiles. "We know what you're thinking. 'How can Mary and Harry possibly know enough about our loved one to write something heartfelt and genuine?' Fair question!"

Mary smiles back at Harry and continues. "You see, here at Mary and Harry's Obituaries, we take the time to get to know the dearly departed. We talk to you, the family. And we listen, really listen. We collect your stories, your anecdotes, your precious memories and then we go back to the office and start writing."

"Since opening last month, we've heard from dozens of satisfied customers," Harry says. "Many have received compliments about the thorough yet sensitive way they—meaning Mary and me, of course—have captured the essence of the deceased. And if the dead could talk, I'm sure we'd have lots more."

They share a disarming chuckle and Harry continues. "'What about money?' you may be thinking. After all, nothing's as certain as death and taxes and even after the former someone still has to pay the latter. Discussing money may seem crass, but it's a necessary discussion."

"That's why we have a price point for every budget," Mary adds. "For those for whom money is no object—"

Harry interrupts. "Or perhaps those who love their family just a little bit more..."

Mary giggles. "Now, Harry, you stop that..."

"Just kidding, folks," Harry says. "That's one thing you'll find here at Mary and Harry's. We don't take ourselves too seriously. Death doesn't have to be all crying and wailing and misery. Sometimes there's a funny side. It releases the pressure. But rest assured, we take *you* seriously."

"Anyways," Mary says, "for those who want to splurge, we have a Luxury package that comes with our exclusive Three Hankie Guarantee. We actually guarantee that at least one mourner will go

Beyond the Passage

through three Kleenex—or comparable brand name product—while reading the obit. Folks, this is the one that keeps our noses in the thesaurus looking for just the right words. Often we'll include appropriate quotations from the greatest writers in literary history, writers such as William Shakespeare, Dostoevsky, Kafka, and Mark Twain. And works such as *Romeo and Juliet*, *War and Peace*, and *The Iliad* and *The Odyssey*, just to name a few.

"For you middle class folk out there—which is most of our clientèle—we have our Standard. The Standard is much like the Luxury in many ways. Authors quoted will include Danielle Steele, Erma Bombeck and JK Rowling. Quoted works include *The Grass is Always Greener Over the Septic Tank*, *Bathroom Humour*, Volumes 3 through 6, and the much beloved Peanuts cartoons."

"Heck of a deal, Mary," Harry says. "And for those on a fixed income with a more modest budget we have a Basic, no-frills plan that offers both dignity and simplicity. All quotes are from the classic volume, *Fish and Dicks*, a collection of, well, unusual material by Jim Prime and Ben Robicheau. This is ideal for those who didn't really care that much for the mournee. Maybe an ex-husband or wife or that uncle who was always asking for money—you know the type. In addition, we will work with you to write your own obituary! This will ensure that your story is told accurately, without leaving it in the hands of an unqualified third party, possibly harbouring a personal grudge."

"The beauty of this is that, for a nominal fee," Mary says, "we will update the text periodically right up until that fatal day. This allows for every last accomplishment to be included. For those who wish to make a convenient one-time payment, we have a lay-away plan."

"So to speak!" Harry says.

Mary pats his arm. "Harry, you stop that right now!" Her smile becomes an earnest look into the heart of the camera. "So come see us, Mary and Harry at Mary and Harry's Obituaries. We put the 'ghost' in 'ghostwriters'. And remember: Tasteful is our middle name. Hope to see you soon!"

Harry switches off the camera and the two high-five.

Jim Prime

A customer enters and approaches the desks. He's wearing a three-piece, pinstriped suit with a crimson red handkerchief peeking from the chest pocket. He looks around, taking it all in.

Harry greets him warmly. "Good morning sir! I'm Harry. This is my wife, Mary."

"Sheldon," the man says, unenthusiastically shaking the proffered hands.

"How may we help you, Sheldon?"

"Uh, yes...that is, I hope so. You write obituaries?"

"We do indeed, sir," Harry says, indicating the sign on the front of his desk. "Were you in need of our services?"

"I might be, yes. I'm a businessman, you see, a numbers man. Never had much of a talent for writing as such. My wife recently passed away and I want to give her a respectful send-off. Wonderful woman."

"Certainly, sir. My condolences. Never easy. In a better place. Too soon. Meet again someday. Gets easier. And all that. Please take a seat."

"Thanks." He sits.

Harry takes a notepad and pen from his desk drawer, writes something at the top of the page and underlines it. "Now, I'm going to have to ask a few questions. I hope that's okay."

Sheldon nods.

"Age of the departed?"

"She was 74."

"Oh, my way too soon," Harry says, writing.

"Cause of death?"

"Is that necessary?"

"It allows us to personalize the obituary, you see, sir. The more information we have, the better. Like if she died skiing, we could work that derring-do into the narrative."

"Can't we just say that she died of natural causes?"

"If you like. May I ask her name?"

"Blanche. Blanche Peacock."

Harry and Mary both look at the customer and Mary puts her hand to her mouth.

Beyond the Passage

"Oh dear. We were just reading about her last night, Mr...Mr. Peacock, I assume."

"One and the same."

Mary struggles to maintain a smile. "Well...the circumstances of your wife's passing were certainly well covered in the press."

"Rumour and innuendo. Sensationalism. Just trying to sell newspapers and make money off someone's grief."

"Yes, well parts of her body were found in three different locations in the county."

"Easily explainable."

"Of course," Harry says. "Sorry, sir, I don't wish to be rude, but haven't you been charged with her murder?"

"Technically, yes. I'm out on bail at the moment. $1.5 million, which I thought was excessive. Luckily, I can afford it."

Mary has recovered and manages a genuine smile. "Yes, Mr. Peacock. We've purchased cars from your dealership on Highway 6."

"Ah yes, that was my first. Just opened my fifth over in Sackville last month."

The door opens and a voluptuous blonde lady leans in. She is chewing gum. She smiles at Harry and Mary and says, "Will you be much longer, Donnie?"

Peacock is slightly irritated. "I'll be along soon. Just wait in the car. Listen to the radio or something."

She leaves abruptly. Harry and Mary exchange glances.

"That was my assistant," Peacock says. "Been with me for years. Very efficient. Now, can you people help me or not? I need an obituary for Blanche. Something that shows my deep love for her and that kind of thing."

Mary shakes her head from side to side and sighs deeply. "I won't lie to you, Mr. Peacock. It's going to be a challenge."

"I'm willing to pay top dollar."

Harry interjects eagerly. "I'm sure we can create something suitable. Tell us a little about your late wife."

"Well, we'd been married for 22 years at the time of her untimely death. We were both very young. The marriage had its ups and downs, but that's hardly unusual, is it? She had affairs. I had af-

Jim Prime

fairs. She ran up huge charges on my platinum card. Of course I wasn't perfect, either."

"In what way?" Mary said.

"I have a temper, I won't deny it. And yes, I happen to love women. So arrest me."

He sees the irony of what he just said and quickly moves on. "The fact is that business has dropped off a bit since my wife's death and the...things that followed. I need someone to write an obituary that shows the real me. How I loved my wife and all that. Customers—that is, people—have to regain their trust in me and my integrity. Otherwise my reputation with the buying public— that is, my dear friends and neighbours—will be ruined."

"I can see your dilemma," Mary says. "Of course, we have a reputation to worry about, too. As a new business, we have to be careful not to get involved in anything shady."

Peacock slams his fist on the desk. "There is nothing shady about Shady Motors. I give the best deals in town and past customers would confirm that. I stand behind my cars, new and used and that's just a fact!"

"Sorry," Mary says. "I certainly didn't mean to imply—"

"Do you want this job or not? I'll pay twice your regular fee."

Mary and Harry look at each other, then Harry turns to Mr. Peacock and stretches out his hand. They shake on the deal.

When their new client has left the office, Mary and Harry set to work writing the most dangerous obituary they'd ever penned. Despite attempts to gain insights from their client and from friends of his late wife, they have to use all their creative skills. Friends and family, it turns out, are much too intimidated to talk, and their client provides scant information about his late wife.

His final instructions were: "Make her sound nice, happy, you know. And play up how much we, you know, loved each other, and all that."

The following week the obituary appears in the Briertown *Gazette*. Mary and Harry had experienced a rare and ultimately fatal attack of conscience.

Beyond the Passage

The obituary begins innocently enough. There are ample references to the departed's accomplishments, her beauty "inside and out," and her generosity to local charitable organizations. It is when the text moves to describing those "left behind to grieve" that not-so-subtle hints of foul play begin to appear. Phrases like "husband Sheldon, well-known auto dealer who makes a living trading old models in for newer ones." And "devoted partner who will be unable to travel anywhere without some small reminder of his wife."

They hope that he won't notice the cryptic clues, but he does. Two weeks later a single two-column obituary of Mary and Harry O'Leary appears in the paper. Because neither Harry nor Mary had any living relatives, a newspaper staffer writes it. It reads as much like a news item as a final tribute.

> Mary and Harry died as a result of injuries received in a car accident. Police have determined that they failed to negotiate a sharp turn on scenic Route 8 which hugs the coast line. The car plunged into the water and they were unable to escape. Preliminary investigation reports leaked to the media determined that the brake fluid in the car had drained out, apparently due to a faulty seal.
>
> Oddly, the car was brand new, having been purchased earlier the same week from Shady Hills Motors during its annual deep-discount sale.

Jim Prime

Amethyst summer

Sea and sky had blended into a gunmetal grey with only a subtle pencil-line of horizon to draw any distinction between the two. It was an unusually warm mid-November morning and already villagers were gathering along the shore to view the aftermath of the gale. The storm had swept up the east coast, gathering momentum over miles of open water before striking the islands with full force.

The moon had been full the previous night and, in answer to the lunar summons, the tide had risen high above the pebbled beach before receding, leaving in its wake a generous variety of offerings. This flotsam and jetsam littered the shoreline as if the ocean had finally had enough of man's slovenly ways and disgorged all the synthetic garbage back at us in disgust. It vomited up cans and bottles and a jumble of plastic containers.

Some of the detritus had no doubt been thrown overboard from small boats, some from ocean liners; regardless of its origins, it was all deposited on the shores of the islands, mixed with various tools of the fishing trade—buoys, nets and snarled lengths of yellow polypropylene rope.

Gales and hurricanes that move up the American east coast often make first landfall on Long and Brier Islands. Situated between two bays, the islands and Digby Neck create a fork in their path, and this time had split the storm into three sections, one veering to the west and up the Bay of Fundy and one to the east into St. Mary's Bay. The middle prong, the islands, not only received the full frontal assault but were scoured on their left and right flanks by the other two sections.

In Freeport, the sea flowed like a raging river through the narrow entrance to the village's usually snug cove. These were not the

Beyond the Passage

steady incremental advances of tide; this was the ocean unleashed from its usual protocols, sucking debris along with it as it funnelled between the wharves and stone breakwater—a parade of fluorescent cork buoys, plastic bottles, driftwood and slats from smashed lobster traps. The rancid contents of a beached gurry scow were strewn along the shoreline.

Above it all, seagulls circled and swooped, looking down as if in judgment at the chaos below. More likely the frenzied scavengers were anticipating the buffet that awaited them above the high water mark.

The confluence of high tides and high winds was more than the breastworks could contain, and the sea poured over these barriers, crossed the road onto lawns, and flooded the basements of homes that hugged the ragged horseshoe of water. In places, the pounding surf undermined the pavement, causing it to collapse into the cove.

In Westport two boats had been ripped from their moorings and deposited onto front yards, where they sat like extravagant lawn ornaments. Other small craft were splintered against the rocks. Thousands of dollars' worth of lobsters were lost when a floating lobster car broke free and grounded itself on Cow's Ledge.

Holly had been there since first light to capture the images. When she arrived, several Cape Islanders, the legendary boats that are the lifeblood of the Islands' fishery, were resting on their sides on the muddy flats alongside the government wharf. Within hours they'd been lifted so high that their decks loomed above the wooden platform. The water rose so rapidly that, from her position on the banks, Holly could keep track of the level by using the rusted iron bars of the wharf ladders as markers.

Supported by rough wooden stilts, the open wharves were overwhelmed by the swells that surged beneath. The planks rose and fell like piano keys and spouts of water shot through the gaps as if synchronized by some other-worldly power.

This was Nature at her most aggrieved, her powerful elements strategically allied as the fearsome North Atlantic joined forces with unrelenting winds to wreak maximum havoc.

Holly's editor back in Boston would be pleased when he saw

Jim Prime

these unexpected additions to her submitted photo files. To her surprise, the inexperienced young photojournalist had been given an assignment from the *Boston Globe* to record the impact of the fishing decline on villages along the coast of New England and the Maritimes. She appreciated the fact that her job not only didn't tie her to a desk, it didn't tie her to a place.

In fact she had only been inside the *Globe* offices on two occasions since her initial interview. The three-week project was officially complete, and this side trip was supposed to be strictly personal. Ironically, it might now rate a feature story of its own.

The storm had been forecast, but few foresaw the last minute change of path that brought it on a collision course with southwestern Nova Scotia.

The adrenaline that had fuelled Holly throughout the long, gruelling day had all but run its course. Long ago she had learned that nature photography was as much a physical endeavour as it was artistic. She suddenly just wanted to return to her bed at the AirBnB that she had checked into late the previous evening after the drive from Bangor, Maine.

She had scarcely fallen asleep that night when the first strong gusts rattled the windows of her small room, jolting her awake. Her slumber after that was fitful as she swam aimlessly through a foreboding sea of indecipherable dreams.

Yes, it was best to shoot the aftermath of the storm in the first light of morning. She drove her Ford Escape around the cove toward the boarding house. As she crossed the small bridge across the brook that emptied into the head of the cove, she passed a pickup truck. The man at the wheel looked familiar.

~

Josh Garron left the repurposed workshop that stood adjacent to his house and jumped in his truck. He had recently converted the building into a small home office. It wasn't fancy, but served his purposes well enough. As a marine biologist and whale researcher he needed ready access to his maps and charts and it wasn't al-

Beyond the Passage

ways convenient to cross the passage to his 'official' office on Brier Island.

Throughout the day, he'd been in almost constant touch with the skipper and crew of the whale watch boat *Cetacean 11*. The vessel seemed to be faring well in the lee of two parallel wharves, and he could now turn his attention to his own boat, which was moored across the cove.

As he passed over the small bridge, ironically known to locals as the Big Bridge, Josh saw a Ford Escape pass by with a woman at the wheel. Cars 'from away' stood out on the island and Josh checked the rear view mirror.

Rattled, he pulled to the side of the road and stopped. With some difficulty, he extracted his cell phone from his pocket and scanned his emails from the past weeks.

Holly's message was there, with the subject line *It's been awhile* and a star indicating that it was important enough to be saved.

His finger hovered over the link for a long moment before he seemed to dismiss the impulse. He hurriedly returned the phone to his pocket and continued on his way.

~

From the age of 12 until she turned 17, Holly spent her summers on these islands, staying with her grandmother, Ida. Each year her parents joined her for the final week of August before they all returned to Boston for the start of school.

After years of trying, her parents, Phil and Lynn, had all but given up on having kids when Lynn became pregnant at the age of 35. Phil was an orthopaedic surgeon at Boston General and Lynn was curator of a small art gallery across the river in Cambridge.

The demands of their jobs made it difficult to get away for any extended period, so when Phil's mother, Ida, suggested that Holly come to Long Island and stay the summer, they embraced the idea, thankful to have a safe haven for their daughter away from the city. Ida's arthritis was growing worse each year and having Holly there to help seemed an ideal arrangement for everyone.

Jim Prime

During these glorious summers, Holly had established a special bond with her grandmother and through her she grew to love everything about the islands. Her parents were loving but overprotective and controlling. She hated the endless series of stuffy social events they insisted she attend with them. For Holly these summer visits represented freedom.

Ida gave her free rein to roam the beaches in search of sea glass, take nature walks along the shore, stay up late and sleep in until mid-morning if she wanted. She seldom did because her days were full of opportunities.

As late June turned to July and July to August, she picked cranberries, strawberries, blackberries, and raspberries and helped to put up preserves. As the years passed she gradually took over many of the gardening duties that Ida could no longer manage. They spent most evenings playing crokinole or marathon games of Forty-fives, and listening to music.

Holly had just turned 15 when she met Josh. His father owned one of Freeport's two general stores and his summer job was to stock shelves, sweep floors, and deliver weekly grocery orders to those unable to get out.

One Friday evening he knocked on Ida's door, and when it opened Holly was standing there. Ida appeared behind her and introduced them with a twinkle in her eye.

Josh was immediately smitten. During the pause that followed, he could feel his face growing red.

Mercifully, Holly's grandmother intervened. "Josh is the young man I told you about, Holly, the one who delivers my groceries every Friday evening. How are your parents, Josh?"

"Good," Josh replied, trying desperately to regain some semblance of cool. "Dad's pretty busy in the store these days, what with the summer people and all. Mom's started painting classes at the high school."

"Good for Evie! Holly is quite an artist, too, you know—"

"Gran!" Holly interrupted.

"Well, you are. I'll bet Josh could show you some new places around the village for you to paint."

Beyond the Passage

"Actually, I'm more into photography these days," she said.

"Well, then, he could show you some places to take your pictures."

"Sure," Josh said. "I could do that."

Holly smiled again. "Okay."

"Okay...well... see you soon, I guess. I'll call you...bye."

Mrs. Conrad closed the door and Josh walked home feeling as if his small world had just grown a bit larger.

That Sunday they went for the first of many long walks along the shore. He knew exactly where he wanted to take her. It was a place he had discovered by accident the previous fall but had returned to many times, always alone.

They walked the half mile to Beautiful Cove, which Holly had already explored a few times, but instead of stopping there, he led her along a stretch of elevated headland that ran eastward from the cove through a thicket of spruce and alders.

When they finally emerged from the woods, they were on a plateau of rock that overlooked the cove and the Bay of Fundy beyond. Josh took her hand and warned her not to look down.

They slowly eased their way down a steep gully until they reached a four-foot-wide rock ledge some twenty feet above the churning water. To their left the ledge appeared to end abruptly about ten feet along, after which there was a five-foot gap.

Holly was surprised when Josh tightened his grip on her hand and moved in that direction. Despite his instructions, she couldn't resist the urge to look down and immediately wished she hadn't. The water was slapping against the razor sharp rocks directly below.

She fixed her eyes on Josh's back and kept them there.

They were almost at the far end of the ledge and it seemed like Josh was about to step off into thin air with her in tow. Instead, he turned left and it was then that Holly spotted the deep fissure in the rock face. The fold in the cliff had been completely invisible until they were almost on top of it.

Josh turned to her and grinned. "Watch your head," he said, and they ducked through the opening.

Jim Prime

The passage was dank and dark and so narrow that they were forced to turn sideways to edge their way along.

They rounded a final turn and were immediately met by an explosion of colour as the cleft opened into a large stone chamber. As her eyes adjusted to the sudden brightness, Holly could see that they were in a ten-by-ten foot cavity in the rock face, open only at the western end. Through the wide aperture she could see far offshore to the horizon but a jutting and jagged shelf of stone blocked the sea below from her view.

The afternoon sun was shining in, illuminating the interior walls. She looked around, dazzled.

They were surrounded on three sides by broad veins of amethyst that zigzagged across the walls of the enclosure. The bands were shades of purple, some delicate lilac, some rich, resplendent violet. They criss-crossed randomly and ran in all directions, but seemed to emanate from a solid iridescent core of reddish-purple amethyst at least four feet square. It was as if a million purple field flowers had been embedded in the rock and were blossoming in the flood of sunlight.

She was speechless. They were inside a natural kaleidoscope that sparkled and danced before their eyes.

~

"We're invisible here," Josh said. "No one can see in. Only the sun when it reaches just the right angle in the western sky. And even the sun only gets one glimpse a day."

He paused. "Please don't tell anyone."

She searched his face expecting to see a mischievous grin but he was serious.

"People would ruin it," he said simply.

She nodded.

Each time that Josh and Holly made a pilgrimage to the amethyst chamber he again swore her to secrecy. The cave took on a special significance for them both. It was a symbol of trust and respect. It was their place, a place of promises and commitments

Beyond the Passage

and solemn secrets.

Their relationship deepened over the next two summers. In the fall and winter they exchanged long letters with cryptic messages that would be parent-proof, just in case.

When she was 17 they made love for the first time. Afterwards they clung tightly to each other as if trying to freeze the moment in time.

When that final summer drew to an end, she returned to New England with her parents as usual. A month passed and he had heard nothing from her. As fall turned to winter, he wrote several letters but they were all returned unopened.

When he asked Ida about it, she was kind but vague. She said they had moved to Cape Cod, and Phil and Lynn now commuted to the city. She gave him the new address—although reluctantly, he thought later.

The following summer came and went with no word from Holly. Ida had closed up her house and her neighbours told him that she would be staying with her son's family for the foreseeable future. Josh assumed that she was ill and under the care of medical specialists in Boston.

The truth was very different. When Holly and her family made their final return to Boston, her mother had taken her for her annual pre-school medical. Following the examination, the doctor had called mother and daughter into his office and delivered the news in even tones. Holly was pregnant.

~

The post-storm sun broke through by noon to reveal a very different world. It was as if landscape and seascape had somehow been melded together and there were elements of one mixed into the other. In the eerie calm, with a warmish breeze now blowing onshore, fishermen gathered at the wharf to smoke and survey the damage.

As he drove past, Josh could imagine the conversations. Years earlier, while talking with another fisherman after yet another

Jim Prime

storm, Josh recalled his father saying, "Yup, that was quite a blow." That was about as demonstrative as most fishermen got.

Josh's boat had ridden out the storm moored in the cove and had suffered only minor damage. His first stop was at the slip near the Legion, where he rowed his punt out to the mooring and bailed it out.

Those who had opted to tie their boats to the wharf had fared far worse and several had been smashed to kindling. He silently vowed to spend the next week lending whatever practical assistance he could to those unfortunate men.

At the western tip of Brier Island, an ancient war canoe was found protruding from an earthen bluff eaten away by the high tides. The find was significant enough to have experts from the Maritime Museum on site the very next day to ensure that it was carefully extracted from the cliff and removed to Halifax.

At the height of the storm, power lines had been snapping and sparking on the seaweed-strewn pavement, but now they lay still. The main power cable that connected the islands to the mainland had broken. The power would remain out for more than a week and islanders were forced to reclaim their dusty kerosene lamps from attics and basements.

Josh spent the rest of the morning and most of the afternoon helping fellow fishermen with makeshift repairs, before slowly guiding his own boat along the shore to assess the damage to fish houses and wharfage. A fisherman salvaging lost fishing gear told him about Holly being back.

He returned to his truck and made one final stop to check on an elderly woman who had lost several shingles from her porch roof. After patching the bare section with a piece of plywood, he covered it with a tarp and nailed it in place. He made a mental note to get some shingles from the Home Hardware in Digby and do a proper repair in a day or so.

It was now late afternoon and his preoccupation with the storm was suddenly replaced by a tempest of thoughts and emotions that had been brewing in his mind and heart. He needed a quiet place to think.

Beyond the Passage

He drove to the end of Lover's Lane, but instead of turning right down the dirt road to Beautiful Cove, he turned left along a muddy path that ran parallel to the entrance to Grand Passage. The old Dodge whined in protest as he manoeuvred it slowly up a steepening grade. Thickets of alder bushes encroached from both sides, slapping against the windshield and screeching along the side of the truck.

He emerged onto an open plateau of land that fronted onto the bay, switched off the ignition and rolled down his window. A light breeze was blowing onshore and he inhaled it greedily.

Ahead of him, directly across the eastern end of Grand Passage, the silhouette of Northern Point stood in sharp relief against the sky.

The fog was lingering far just beyond the point and, as if on cue, a series of other-worldly mating calls shattered the silence. The sonorous, two-syllable blast from the Peter's Island Light foghorn was answered by a single mournful wail from Northern Point. The fainter drone of Western Light could be heard joining in from the opposite side of the island, a background bass note of support for the trio. *The three tenors*, the locals called them.

Though the weather didn't really warrant their warnings, these familiar sounds were somehow reassuring to Josh, signalling a return to normalcy.

He sat there for a long time as if trying to make a decision. He checked his cell phone and carefully re-read Holly's email. Finally he started the truck and slowly drove back down the narrow path.

~

Holly had risen early from a short but refreshing sleep and had retraced her steps from the previous day's shoot, trying hard to take as many pictures as possible from similar vantage points. The contrasts from frantic last minute preparations for the gathering storm, to mid-storm fury, to post-storm calm would be striking. The day had grown clear and bright as if Mother Nature was over her tantrum and was apologizing for her unruly behaviour.

Jim Prime

Holly had also finished her day's work and as the sun dipped lower in the sky she had a sudden urge to drive to Beautiful Cove.

She parked the SUV at the end of the lane and walked to the beach. The sweet fragrance of wild roses reached her nose and immediately took her back to a Sunday afternoon years earlier, her last summer on the islands. The last time she had seen Josh. The day was bright and clear and only the distant church bell disturbed the stillness.

Just then a low rumble roused her from her reverie and she looked up to see a pickup truck driving down the road toward her, leaving a trail of dust behind it. The truck came to a stop and she raised her hand to shade her eyes against the sun. The door opened.

~

Back in Boston, Holly's parents had settled on a plan, without input from Holly. Phil and Lynn were devout Catholics, so a termination was out of the question. She would continue with school as long as possible and then remain at home until the birth. After the baby was born, Ida would come to Boston and help out. Meanwhile the parents would continue to carry on as usual. It was important that they keep up their social obligations. Naturally, secrecy would have to be maintained until an out-of-state adoption could be arranged.

Physically, Holly's pregnancy proceeded smoothly. Emotionally she was a wreck, afraid and wracked with guilt. Despite her parents' careful planning and her aunt's gentle reassurances, she felt alone and abandoned, even though it was she who had left Josh.

She wondered about him, and the urge to pick up the phone and call him was almost unbearable. But in the end it was always easier just go with the flow and let someone else decide.

When the baby was born, Holly finally found her voice. She was firm. There would be no further talk of adoption. She would raise the child on her own if need be.

She needn't have worried, because everyone immediately fell in love with the little girl whom Holly had named Amy.

154

Beyond the Passage

When Amy was two years old, a colleague of Holly's father dropped by. He was in his final year of residency at Boston General and he and Holly fell into a long conversation that lasted long after her parents had gone to bed. Soon he was visiting every weekend. He was good looking and ambitious and seemed not the least bit deterred by the presence of the toddler.

Phil and Lynn encouraged the relationship and although guilt still gnawed at Holly, she convinced herself that Amy would benefit from a male figure in her life. When he proposed she said yes. It seemed like a sensible solution and Holly's parents assured her that she was doing the right thing.

Right for Holly, right for the baby. Even right for Josh. Best he never knows, they said. Why fracture his life, too?

~

The day that Josh got word of Holly's marriage he had felt a sinking sensation in the pit of his stomach. As time passed, anger pushed aside the sadness, and then even the anger dissipated, leaving only memories, some bitter and some sweet.

Each passing year Holly faded a bit more from his thoughts. He met and married Susan, a girl from Digby. They moved to Halifax, where he studied at the Bedford Institute of Oceanography. They settled into a comfortable routine and life was good.

Following graduation, he worked as a researcher at the Department of Fisheries. They wanted children, but after two miscarriages decided it wasn't meant to be.

They'd been married for just over two years when she started experiencing severe headaches. Within six months she was dead of a brain tumour.

When he learned about an opening for a researcher for BIOS, a joint Canadian-American whale study initiative on Brier Island, he applied for and got the position. He moved back to the islands and immediately bought a used Cape Islander to fish from in his spare time.

Once back on the islands, memories of Holly came flooding back,

155

Jim Prime

but now only the good times. Every place he went reminded him of her.

~

Holly and Paul soon discovered that, aside from Amy, they had little in common. Paul was consumed with his professional life and intent on continuing his diabetes research. He was often away at conferences or working late hours in the lab. This left little time for a home life. When he was home, he was often impatient with Holly and distant with Amy. Holly was left to raise her daughter on her own.

When an offer was made for Paul to come to Seattle as Director of Diabetic Research at Washington State University, he accepted on the spot, without discussing it with Holly. For weeks they argued bitterly about the move and, after several long talks and a disastrous meeting with a marriage counsellor, Paul filed for divorce. Holly didn't contest it.

Amy was sad for the next few weeks but, soon her cheerful nature won out.

~

Holly had planned to contact Josh even before the *Globe* assignment. With surprisingly little effort, she had found his email address and emailed him, hitting send quickly before she could change her mind.

The message had been short and to the point. She said she was going to be in the area on business and would love to see him if he had the time. She added that she would understand if he declined but that she "owed him an explanation" and hoped he'd agree to see her.

He had written back. "Give me a call when you arrive."

Now that the moment had arrived, the task ahead seemed impossible. This wasn't fair to Josh. How could she possibly face him?

~

Josh got out of the truck and they greeted each other almost shyly, as if they were awkward teenagers again.

They embraced, at first haltingly and then with a familiarity that surprised them both. The years had changed them physically but they were seeing each other through a filter that erases time.

"Let's walk," said Josh.

Only a few words passed between them as they hiked toward their secret hideaway. As they drew closer, they could see the sheer cliff face that held the enclosure.

Suddenly they stopped in their tracks. At the bottom of the cliff was a pile of large rocks and rubble. The high tides and relentless pounding of the waves had washed away the sand and undercut the base, causing layer upon layer of shale to collapse. The protruding shelf that led into the opening had lost its support and crashed into the sea.

The amethyst deposits were exposed for the first time. Even as they watched, the sun caught the amethyst and reflected it back to them in a blaze of colour.

The secret that they had shared and protected, their secret, was there for all to see. There would be worthy efforts by some villagers to protect the site, but before long scavengers would arrive to remove the stones, ripping them from their settings with pick axes and whatever other crude instruments were at hand. They would cart them away to tacky gift shops and upscale boutiques, leaving only ugly scars in the rock. The remaining pieces would be ostentatiously displayed on island mantelpieces and window sills.

"We knew it couldn't last forever. You kept my secret well," he said. "I'm proud of you."

She turned from him. "Yes, I'm very good at keeping secrets," she said.

A tear rolled down her cheek and she quickly wiped it away. "Sometimes secrets bring you together, sometimes they tear you apart."

He looked at her.

"I've kept a secret from you for a long time and that's unforgiv-

Jim Prime

able. I've been a coward."

Before she could gather herself to continue, Josh interrupted. "You know, I lost a wonderful friend when your grandmother passed away. She was a very wise woman.'"

Holly looked at him quizzically.

"After you left I avoided her for quite a while. Brought back too many memories, I guess. But one evening after I moved back from Halifax I was passing her place and decided to drop in and say hello. It was a bit awkward at first but, before we knew it, we were talking a blue streak, just like old times. After that it became a weekly thing. I'd drop by pretty much every week right up to the time she had her first stroke. I'd do some chores for her, maybe run an errand or two, then we'd sit at the kitchen table and drink tea and talk about all kinds of things. She had a great memory about how the village used to be back in the day.

"Once in a while she'd mention some piece of news about you and your new family. Just casually, you know? 'By the way, Holly and Paul just moved to a new apartment.' That kind of thing. Then she started showing me pictures. Never of you. Never of your husband. Just pictures of your little girl. She was just a toddler at the time. At first I thought it was just something that all proud grandmothers do because she doted on Amy."

Holly smiled. "She did."

"It took me a while. Guess I'm not the sharpest hook on the line. As time passed, she showed me more pictures of this little girl. It kind of bothered me at first, to be honest, like she was deliberately trying to hurt me. It wasn't like her to be, you know, insensitive like that. And then one evening it finally sank in. She showed me a picture of Amy taken at an ice cream stand near a beach. She was wearing a shirt that said Daddy's Girl."

"Dennisport, on Cape Cod. We went every summer after..." Her voice trailed off.

"The funny thing is I didn't see me in her at all. I looked at her and saw my mother. She looked a lot like my mother. Don't know how I didn't see it right away. Just some expression on her face. Of course, I didn't let on, and we never really talked about it, but Ida

158

Beyond the Passage

could see that I had finally caught on. It was an act of kindness, not cruelty. She told me the secret without actually telling me."

"And then, a few months later, I heard about your marriage break-up, through Ida. That's when she told me everything. About your parent's threats, about your desperation, everything."

"So you've known for...three months?"

"About that. Enough time to think about it. In fact I've thought of little else."

"And you didn't contact me?"

"I had a feeling I'd hear from you."

Josh had been staring at the cove as he spoke but now he turned to face her and saw that she still had tears in her eyes. "Does she know?" he said.

Holly took a deep breath and let it out. "Yes. I told her a few days before I left on this trip. I told her everything."

"How did she handle it?"

"The thing is, I would have told her long ago if not for mom and dad. They were wonderful parents in many ways, but they completely ran my life, and I let them. They wanted to protect me—and maybe themselves—from scandal. The odd thing is that my grandmother wasn't at all scandalized. I couldn't have gotten through it all without her. She was there throughout the pregnancy and she was a kind of buffer between me and my parents.

"I think Amy always suspected that something wasn't quite right. She's a bright girl. When I spoke of her father, the stories didn't quite fit with Paul's personality. Paul could be so gruff and impatient. Sometimes...when she asked me about her father and how we met, I may have mixed in large parts of Josh Garron along with Paul. Little things, like your smile, or what made you laugh... or some of the places you took me."

Josh looked at her with a sudden realization. "You told Amy about the amethyst cave, didn't you?"

"Yes, I told her that her father had taken me to a place that no one else in the world had ever been. The most beautiful place. I didn't think you'd mind."

"Not a bit. Thank you for that," he said quietly.

Jim Prime

"But how did you know I told Amy?" she said.

The faint clanging of a far-off bell buoy broke the long silence that followed.

"Your grandmother got a letter from Amy. She stuck it to her refrigerator and I noticed it during a visit. It had 'I love you' scrawled in block letters at the top and under that there was a drawing of a giant yellow sun with its rays shining across the blue sea into a big hole in a wall of rock. Inside there was a rainbow of colours. She must have used every crayon in the box.

"I asked Ida about it, but she just said that Amy had a terrific imagination. I mentioned that I liked it and when I left she gave it to me. I made a little frame for it and hung it on my kitchen wall. It's still there."

Holly grew quiet, searching her memory. "I remember!" she said. "When she was about five or six, she was obsessed with a cartoon character called Rainbow Brite. She slept with that doll every night and I must have read the book to her a thousand times at bedtime. It was about a world that was always grey until the heroine used her magic to flood it with colour.

"One night when I finished the book Amy got very quiet. I asked what was wrong and she said she wished it was real. That's when I told her about the amethyst chamber. I told her that once her dad had once taken me to a magical place that no one else had ever seen before. Where all the colours of the rainbow were trapped in the grey rock, making it glitter and sparkle. I wanted her to know that her father could make magic like that. But I had no idea that she had sent it..."

She smiled at the memory. "Of course I swore her to secrecy."

They laughed.

Josh looked out over the bay where the western sky had added brilliant streaks of purple that were reflected in the dark corduroy sea. "If only..." he said.

"If only what?"

He pointed toward the water's edge. "That's the limit of my world, right here, Holly. Yours is limitless."

"That's funny, I think this island is the freest place I've ever

Beyond the Passage

been."

"Some would say it's a great place to visit, but they could never live here. They can't wait to get on that ferry and head back home."

"I feel sorry for those people. This isn't a place to leave, it's a place to come home to."

Jim Prime

Finally, Finley

Clickety-clack, clickety-clack, clickety-clack. The long, black train was struggling to make it to the top of a high hill. *Clickety-clack, clickety-clack.* The hill was getting steeper and steeper and the train was going slower and slower. *Clickety-clack.* And steeper...and slower. *Clickety...* It was almost at the top.

Suddenly the clickety-clacks turned into sharp *tap, tap, taps.*

Must be a problem with the engine, Finley thought.

The sound came again, this time louder: *Tap, Tap, Tap.* In the distance, he heard someone call his name. "Finley!"

They must need my help to fix the engine, he thought.

He rolled over and pulled the covers over his head.

"Finley Hendrix Canton!!"

He woke with a start! Someone was knocking on his bedroom door and calling his name. It was his mother. Finley had been lying in his nice warm bed, dreaming about trains. In his dream, he was the engineer. Finley was always the engineer in his dreams.

"It's 8:15. You're going to be late for school!" his mom said.

"Just a minute," Finley said sleepily.

He yawned and stretched. Slowly, he swung his legs over the edge of the bed and sat there, wiping the sleep from his eyes. The morning sunlight was streaming through his window.

"You haven't even had breakfast yet!" It was his mom again. Her voice was rising.

"Okay, I'm coming."

"Finally, Finley!" said his mother when he arrived at the kitchen table. "No time to lose. Now eat your breakfast."

She put his cereal on the table in front of him. It was his favourite brand, the one in the shape of train cars.

Beyond the Passage

He examined each one carefully. Then he lined them up on his napkin like a long train before finally spooning them into his mouth one by one. When he was finished, he nibbled at the edges of his piece of toast until he had made it into the shape of a caboose. Then he gobbled it down in one bite with a glass of orange juice.

At last, Finley had finished his breakfast.

"Finally, Finley!" his mom said.

He put on his jacket and baseball cap and kissed his mother goodbye.

She said, "Now hurry up or you're going to miss the school bus."

When he got outside, the yellow bus was pulling out from the stop. The driver saw Finley and stopped. She opened the door to let him in, then smiled and shook her head. "Finally, Finley!" she said. "I thought you weren't coming to school today."

As he walked down the aisle of the bus, the rest of the kids all shouted together, "Finally, Finley!" Finley just grinned. He was used to it.

"If you were a train you'd be the caboose, because a caboose is always last to arrive," his friend Ben said.

At school, he was the last one to get off the bus. On the way to class he stopped to look at the drawings on the bulletin board in the hall. Then he stopped to get some water from the fountain.

By the time he came into the classroom, his teacher, Mrs. Penny, had already started math class. "Finally, Finley!" she said.

She had her hands on her hips and was tapping her left foot impatiently. "Please take your seat and help us solve the math problem on page ten."

At the end of the school day, Mrs. Penny made an announcement. "Tomorrow will be a very special day. Mr. John McLintock will be visiting our class. He was a railway man for over forty years before he retired. He's going to tell us all about railroads and trains."

All the kids were very excited, especially Finley. He knew more about trains than any of his friends. "Oh boy," he said to Ben as they got on the bus together. "I can't wait for tomorrow!"

Jim Prime

That night Finley once again dreamed about driving a locomotive. This time two trains were racing each other side by side along two sets of tracks. Finley's train passed the finish line just ahead of the other. He heard people clapping for him and calling his name. *"Clap, clap, clap. Finley, Finley, Finley."*

"Finley!"

He woke up with a jerk and realized that the sound was *tap, tap, tap* and not *clap, clap, clap*. It was his mom again, knocking on his bedroom door.

"Finley, please get up right now!" she said wearily.

Finley's dad was at the breakfast table when he came into the kitchen. "Finally, Finley," he said.

While Finley ate his yogurt and eggs, his dad spoke to him seriously. "This has to stop, Fin," he said. "Your mom and I have to get to our work on time. That's why we've made a time schedule so that we're both here when you leave for school and one of us is here when you get home. When you're late, it makes us late too. And if we don't get to work on time, it affects many other people. It's important for you to be more responsible."

Finley listened and said he would try to do better, but he really didn't see the problem.

He reached the bus stop just as the doors of the bus were closing. The bus driver saw him and opened the door. She smiled but the smile was smaller than yesterday's smile. She said, "Finley, when you're late you make all the kids on the bus late too. And other kids at other bus stops are waiting for me."

Finley said that he was sorry, but didn't think it was a big deal.

~

Finley made it into the classroom just in time to hear Mrs. Penny introduce Mr. McLintock. He was very old and very nice. He had snow white hair and used a cane. He was wearing the uniform and blue and white striped engineer's hat that he used to wear when he worked for the railway.

The kids gathered around Mr. McLintock as he told them stories

Beyond the Passage

about some of the trains he had worked on. He told them about how he started out as a teenager, sweeping the floors at the railway station after school. Then he worked in the summer in the ticket office, helping the ticket-master sell tickets. Over the years, he had worked as a flag man, a brakeman, a fireman, and a signal man. He was a trainmaster and then a yardmaster. Finally, after many years, he became an engineer.

He told them about how the trains worked, and how the tracks were first built through mountains and across rivers. He told them about the old days when trains ran on steam and coal.

When he had finished talking, the kids all clapped. Finley clapped loudest of all.

Mr. McLintock asked them if they had any questions. Several hands shot up. Finley's was higher than all the rest but Mr. McLintock pointed to Lucy, a tall girl with bright red hair.

"How old were you when you started working on the railway?" she said.

"I was 16 years old. I knew nothing about trains. Oh, I thought I did, but I had a lot to learn."

"What kinds of things?" the girl said.

"I had to learn about the different kinds of trains cars and engines and everything I could about the railroad. I knew I wanted to make a career out of it. That's why I had so many jobs."

Mr. McLintock looked around the class and saw Finley's hand still raised. "Okay, young man, I have some questions for *you*. What's the last car on a train called?"

"The caboose," Fin said.

"And the first car?"

"The engine. That's why they call the driver the engineer."

"Very good, very good indeed!" Mr. McLintock said.

Finley already knew a lot about those things. He had read lots of books about trains. He had watched TV shows about them. He had model trains at home. He was feeling very happy.

"Want to know the most important thing I learned about the railroad?" the old man said.

"Yes!" said the class, all at once.

165

Jim Prime

"Of all the things I learned, the biggest thing was how to make the passengers happy."

Finley was surprised. He knew about throttles, and coal cars and freight cars, and cabooses and railway crossings, but he didn't know anything about passengers. Or how to keep them happy.

He put his hand up again. Mr. McLintock said "Yes, young man?"

Finley said "How do you make the passengers happy?"

"Well," Mr. McLintock said, "there are many ways. You always try to be polite and courteous. You know how to answer their questions. You make sure the cars are clean and comfortable. And then there's the biggest thing of all."

"What's that?" Finley asked.

"Get them where they need to go on time! People depend on the railway to get them where they are going safely, and on time. People don't want to be late for work. They don't want to be late meeting their friends. They don't want to be late for appointments with the doctor or dentist. There are many, many reasons that people need to be on time. Trains have to be reliable. People have to trust them."

He paused for a moment and then added proudly, "They used to call me 'Tick Tock' McLintock. People used to set their watches by my arrival and departure times."

Finley was listening carefully. "So the trains have to go really fast, right?"

"Not always. They have to be punctual and dependable," Mr. McLintock said. "That means the railroad has to have a plan and everybody involved has to stick to it. It's called a schedule. They have to plan ahead so each train is sure to be at a certain place at a certain time. Going too fast can be dangerous because there are other trains that use the tracks, too. And going too slow doesn't work, either. So they have to figure out what is reasonable. Then they have to be able to stick to the schedule and not let people down."

He looked around at all the students. "I learned my lesson when I was still very young. I was late getting to work one day there was a long line of people waiting for tickets. The train was held up and

Beyond the Passage

many people were upset. I felt like I had let them down. It was a bad feeling and I didn't want it to happen again."

"What about freight trains?" a boy in the back asked. "They don't have any passengers."

"Schedules are just as important to them. They have to arrive when they are supposed to. They may be carrying freight to a ship that leaves at a certain time. Or fruit and vegetables that have to be fresh. Or maybe a factory needs lumber to keep the workers busy. If it doesn't arrive, people's jobs are in danger."

At recess, Finley sat on a playground swing, thinking about what Mr. McLintock had said. During lunch in the school cafeteria, he thought some more. He even thought about it when he should have been paying attention in science class.

He thought about it as he walked to the bus for the trip back home—and almost missed the bus again.

The kids chanted "Finally, Finley!" when he walked to his seat, but he hardly noticed. He thought about what the railway man had said all the way home on the bus.

That night at the dinner table, he was quieter than usual. His father asked what was wrong.

"Just thinking," Finley said.

"What are you thinking about, Fin?" his dad said.

"Trains and stuff."

"I couldn't do without the train," his father said, finishing the last of his coffee.

"Me either," his mom added with a smile.

"Really?" Finley said.

"Of course," his dad said. "I depend on them to get me to my office on time and to get me home to my family as quickly as possible."

"And I depend on the subway train to get to me my job at the hospital," his mom said. She was a doctor.

The next morning Finley's mom knocked on his door and said "Finley!" There was no answer.

She opened his door and peeked in. The bed was empty. No Finley.

Jim Prime

She went to the kitchen. Finley was sitting at the table, eating his toast and cereal and sipping his orange juice. He had a piece of paper in front of him.

"What's that Fin?" she asked.

"It's my schedule. I made it last night before I went to sleep."

The piece of lined paper said:

Fin's Schedule

8:00 – Get out of bed and get dressed
8:05 – Wash face, etc.
8:15 – breakfast
8:40 – brush teeth
8:45 – catch the bus to school
3:00 – catch the bus home

"Do you think this is a reasonable schedule, mom?" he asked.

"Hmmm, let me see," she said, looking over his shoulder to read it.

"It's a great start, but I don't think you've left yourself enough time for some things. What if your dad or I are in the bathroom and you are a few minutes late? That doesn't leave much time for breakfast, and then everything else gets messed up. Why don't you get up just a bit earlier? Then you won't have to rush."

"That makes sense," Finley admitted. "I'll just go to bed a little earlier."

That night, Fin went to bed a half hour earlier than usual. He got out of bed a half hour earlier the next morning, too. He finished his breakfast and went out to the bus stop. Some of the other kids were there too. It felt good not to have to rush.

When the bus arrived and the door swung open, Finley was the first one to get on.

The bus driver said, "Well, good morning Finley!" Her smile was bigger than he'd ever seen.

The other kids didn't know what to say, so they just said, "Hi, Finley," and, "Good morning, Finley."

Beyond the Passage

It felt good.

Finley was also one of the first to get off the bus when it arrived at school. He walked through the halls quickly, without dawdling.

When Mrs. Penny came into the classroom, Fin was already in his seat with his math book open. She gave him a surprised look and began the lesson.

Finley made some changes to his schedule so that it worked even better. He was proud to be on time for breakfast. It was great to not have to hurry. He was happy to spend some time with his friends before the bus arrived. He liked being ready to go when school started.

Everyone noticed the big change in Fin. His mother and father were happy. The school bus driver was happy. His teachers all smiled and said *Good morning* to him when they came into the classrooms. His friends noticed most of all. He was always on time to play basketball at recess and soccer after school.

Finally, Finley was on time.

Jim Prime

The perfect ending

Writers are always looking for the perfect ending. It's their white whale, if you will, although I'm not sure "Moby-Dick" had a perfect ending, at least not for Captain Ahab.

A perfect ending is elusive. Certainly other literary elements are important too, like a spellbinding first chapter and a plot line that flows like a mighty river with surprises waiting around every bend. But the ending, oh the ending! The ending can be a like a stretch of white water followed by a plunge over the falls or it can lead to the mouth of the river and a vast sea of adventures beckoning from the horizon.

It's all up to the writer.

Quentin Sollows hit the *print* button and within seconds several sheets of paper fell into the tray. He tossed them into the desk drawer with the numerous other pages that represented the 56 other endings he had completed in the past year. He had penned an average of four endings per novel.

But, of late, there had been no complete novels, only endings.

Through the open window of his second-story flat on Queen Street West he could hear the sounds of revelry that are a regular part of Saturday night in this bohemian Toronto enclave. The bar opposite his apartment featured a line of people that stretched from the door down the sidewalk to the corner. The noises ebbed and flowed every time a lucky group was admitted, and cheers went up whenever anyone exited.

Writing is a solitary endeavour and Quentin was, in essence, a solitary man. Not cause and effect, though. At least, not in that order.

Beyond the Passage

He had always been socially awkward, and avoided people whenever possible. Writing was his refuge as well as his passion, and he was good at it. He had written two published books and several magazine articles. His debut novel had even rated a review in the *New York Times* and those royalties had kept him going for more than a year. The *Times* and *Macleans Magazine* acclaimed him as an up-and-comer, someone to keep your eye on. Truth be told, he quite enjoyed the attention so long as people didn't intrude.

Critics and the buying public had largely ignored his second book. He blamed the subject matter. Making his hero a homeless man was a commercial mistake. Torontonians didn't want to feel guilty about a circumstance that confronted them every day of the year, he later surmised in a rare moment of reflection. Or was it rationalization?

Certainly the critics disagreed. They blamed the writing, specifically the ending. The novel had offered much but failed to deliver the goods. "Novel sizzles and then fizzles," wrote the acerbic Roy Clarke in the *Globe and Mail*.

Before long, only the magazine articles that he continued to sell kept him going, and even they were getting fewer and farther between. His agent no longer returned his calls, and there were rumours in the literary world that he had gone quite mad.

Time passed, and eventually the reading public had all but forgotten the once-promising prospect. His earnings scarcely covered the rent on his pricey apartment.

Quentin didn't have writer's block, exactly. After painstaking practice, he could now write an ending at the drop of a hat. Great endings, too. Definitive denouements, epic epilogues, carefully crafted conclusions, fantastic finales, resolute resolutions, and cunning culminations. He wrote tragic endings, happy endings, and suspenseful endings. In short, he had perfected the art of the perfect ending.

He was obsessive about it. Seldom did he even think about the beginnings any more, or the middle bits. In fact, there was just enough plot in his writing to set up a classic finish.

Publishers now praised his final chapters but continued to re-

Jim Prime

ject his numerous submissions due to the mediocrity of those chapters leading up to them.

His mental health continued to deteriorate and in recent months his focus had begun to narrow even further. At first it was final chapters, then the final few pages, final page, final paragraph and final sentence.

The perfect final sentence became his white whale. The quintessential last word was his holy grail. The very thought made him quiver with excitement.

When he picked up a book by some other author, he always turned to the back and read the last few pages. They rarely met with his approval. Quentin had become something of a connoisseur of endings. He was an insufferable snob on the subject.

In his spare time he explored literary classics with the goal of improving the endings. Margaret Mitchell's *Gone with the Wind* ended with, "After all, tomorrow is another day." This irritated him no end, that an epic book about the defining moment in American history, a story that touched on slavery, the loss of countless lives, the splitting of families, should end with such a banality.

He re-wrote it to say, "There shall be no tomorrow for me." After which Scarlet blows her brains out at the door and Rhett looks back, cocks his fancy hat, and keeps walking. *What a powerful commentary about white southern privilege and a changing society*, he thought.

The money from his first blockbuster had dribbled to a pittance, and his very specific writing obsession was not paying the bills. One evening while re-writing the final scenes of *The Grapes of Wrath*, he came up with the idea of advertising his talent for fashioning endings on a popular writing web site.

To his surprise, he received a flood of responses from frustrated novelists who just couldn't seem to complete their opus to their own—or their publisher's—satisfaction. He had found a way to monetize his new talent.

Unsolicited manuscripts arrived daily via UPS and Purolator. They clogged his in-box and if he'd had a transom, they would no doubt have flooded through that as well.

Beyond the Passage

He was churning out endings at an alarming rate. His clients were delighted with his work and word spread quickly throughout the close-knit writing community.

Quentin was making money for the first time in a long time. Big money. He quickly became known in the industry as the Plastic Surgeon because he had saved so many novels from rejection with his flawlessly transplanted textual terminations.

One day he received a manuscript from a well-known writer—let's call him Stephen K.—who had won several prestigious awards and was the toast of the literati. However, like Quentin, his last few novels had landed with a thud and he was desperate to salvage his reputation. His latest manuscript had been rejected due to weak and anti-climactic endings. A mutual friend had recommended Quentin, who was only too happy to help.

The novel was good—very good, in fact—but the final chapter seemed to negate all the writerly flourishes that had come before. The brilliantly crafted story line would be squandered all the reader would remember would be the uninspired ending. The publisher, who up to then thought he had a sure best-seller on this hands, compared it to putting a Kia body on a finely tuned Rolls Royce. The ending just kind of petered out along with the reader's interest.

Quentin received the manuscript on a Friday afternoon and by noon on Monday he had worked his magic. He took a taxi downtown and hand-delivered it to Stephen.

"I think I've fixed your novel," he said as they sipped lattes in Stephen's penthouse apartment. "All it needed was a smoother, more contemplative transition, a few well-placed paragraphs that relate back to the protagonist and remind the readers of her struggles and how she overcame them. Much more satisfying."

"That's great," Stephen replied. "Can't wait to see what you've done."

Quentin said, "The actual changes were not difficult, or even all that original. But the ending is now perfect. I can almost guarantee your book will be a runaway best-seller."

He put a sheet of paper on the coffee table. "Here's your invoice."

Jim Prime

Within a year the book was Number One on several bestsellers' lists. Of course, the author, Stephen, received all the praise, all the accolades, all the interview requests—and, beyond Quentin's one-time payment, all the financial benefits.

Over the next decade, a who's who of popular writers made their way to his door: Atwood, Follett, Rowling, Patterson, to name just a few. Each and every one left with a superb ending and a book that would become a best seller.

Of course, Quentin continued to get none of the credit. That was a strict contractual condition of his hiring. His name was not to be mentioned at all anywhere in the book's credits or acknowledgements. Quentin was anonymous, a ghost writer of endings.

For a while he was satisfied in knowing that he had helped produce stories that people would read and enjoy for years to come. And the money was tremendous. He was now a wealthy man. But still...what would be his epitaph?

> *Quentin Sollows, 56, died yesterday at his home in downtown Toronto. Mr. Sollows had no family and no real friends. His career as a writer peaked when he was 26 and, sadly, he wrote nothing of consequence after that.*

He shuddered at the thought. With every successful project, he grew more resentful. Jealousy raged within him and consumed him. He had helped to create many of the new century's most popular works and no one even knew his name.

One night, while writing another spellbinding ending for John Grisham, he got to thinking. *Why can't I apply what I've learned about perfect endings to my actual life?*

After all, what is a life but a long novel with lots of twists and turns and plot lines?

The more Quentin thought about it, the more convinced he was that he could create an ending for his life that would grab the attention of the world.

He set about mapping out an ending that would astound, an ending that would make him the envy of his fellow writers and

Beyond the Passage

generate an obituary that would, in itself, be a masterpiece.

He planned it for months. Every detail had to be perfect. By pulling some strings, he managed to finagle an invitation to the largest and most prestigious literary festival in North America, the Toronto Book Fest.

He got all his affairs in order, and when the evening of the festival finally arrived, he donned his rented tux and took a limousine downtown to the Grand Hotel. All the great authors were in attendance.

His plan was to stride onto the stage just as the emcee finished his introductory remarks and, before anyone could stop him, reveal that he, and he alone, had written the endings to at least a dozen blockbuster novels. He would point at each of the Goldie Prize nominees in attendance and quote from the endings he had written, before saying in a loud and clear voice, "I wrote that!" One by one, the writers would shrink back into their plush chairs as gasps filled the room.

And then, as the awestruck audience gazed at him with new-found respect, he would take a gun from the inside pocket of his tux and kill himself right there in front of his fellow writers and their devoted readers.

What a statement it would be. What a ticket to immortality. It would be on the front pages of the *Globe and Mail*, the *National Post*, the *Toronto Star*!

Not only would he enhance his own standing but he would tarnish the others' at the same time. And they certainly deserved it. Sitting there with their smug smiles, sharing inside jokes with one another.

He was seated at a table at the back of the huge banquet hall with lesser lights of the business: agents, copy editors and sales people. He studiously ignored them all. The luminaries occupied the front tables and that's where the attention was focused. Waiters fussed around their tables while authors, publishers, reviewers, and media types absorbed the spotlight.

With some difficulty, Quentin finally got a waiter's attention and ordered two double rum and cokes. When they arrived he drank

Jim Prime

them quickly, one after the other.

The show was about to get underway.

His speech, neatly folded in his jacket pocket, was designed to rock the literary establishment to the core. In many ways he felt it was his finest work. A living obituary that would be quoted and re-quoted, somehow subtle and sensational at the same time. Poignant and powerful. A reflection of his life and his pursuit of ex-cellence. It was only fitting that his ending would also be his defin-ing moment.

Of course, timing was of the essence. He only had one chance. He would walk quickly to the stage and commandeer the micro-phone from the host. Before the security people could respond, he would begin to read his final finale—although he didn't really need to read it. He knew it by heart. He was convinced that, once he started, everyone would want to hear every word.

He had a sudden urge to urinate. Those two drinks may have been a mistake. Fortunately, he still had time. He left the table and proceeded to the washroom, conveniently located near his table.

And that's where they found him two days later. In the far left cubicle, sitting on the toilet. Dead of an apparent heart attack.

A brief item appeared in the *Toronto Sun* just opposite the Sun-shine Girl and next to a story about illegal dog fights.

> *Quentin Sollows, 56, died recently in a washroom at the Grand Hotel, during the Toronto Book Fest. Mr. Sollows had no family and no real friends. His career as a writer peaked when he was 26 and, since then, he had not written another word. A truly pathetic ending for a once-promising young novelist.*
>
> *Funeral arrangements are pending.*

Beyond the Passage

Jim Prime

Acknowledgements

I couldn't have completed this book without the help and support of many people.

My fellow writers in various writing groups were invaluable. Susan Haley, who taught writing classes through the Acadia Lifelong Learning Program, was always supportive and encouraging and had a great ear for what works and what doesn't. (She also taught me when and when not to use the word 'enormity.') Thanks to all those at the Writers of the Round Table, who critiqued my writing, almost always gently, occasionally firmly, and always honestly. Thanks to Rachel Cooper for coffee, conversation, and advice.

Another of my writing groups, which we called the Sobey's Sessions because that's where we held our weekly meetings ("Clean up in aisle 3"), offered the chance to share stories and get honest feedback from friends and colleagues. There was no designated group leader but Matt Clairmont soon emerged as our *de facto* leader. Matt is a talented writer, editor and publisher who is destined for big things in each of those areas.

Thanks to the editors at Gage Publishing and Nelson Canada who taught me so much, especially Shari Siamon, Joe Banel, and Rivka Cranley.

I also benefited greatly from workshop sessions with novelist Donna Morrissey, who is a fellow islander from a different island, Newfoundland.

Thanks to my wife, Glenna, for always being there when I needed a push, a word of encouragement, a cuppa coffee, a slice of peanut butter pie, a great new idea, or a reason not to quit. None of this would have happened without her. Thanks to Margaret and

Jim Prime

Catherine for their constant help and inspiration. Also, thanks Dave, Fin, Sam, Jeff and Jung. I love you all. And thanks to Sophie, Luna, and Juno for that most underrated of writers' needs—the distraction.

Thanks to the numerous sports book editors I've worked with over the years, some of whom I've yet to meet face to face but feel I know. All had different approaches but all worked to get the most from me. It's because of you that I have such great respect for the editing profession.

Thanks to Kings Theatre for allowing me to stretch my wings by writing short plays for their unique Festival of Ten Minute Plays, The Kings Shorts.

Thanks to those readers who have shared their thoughts on my writing over the years. Yours are the most important voices of all, and rest assured: they are heard.

Without Ted Williams I would probably never have had the confidence to write for publication. If a baseball fan like me couldn't be inspired to write with and about the greatest hitter who ever lived, he or she should probably consider another line of work. The same applies to Paul Henderson, another true sportsman who has been generous and inspirational; and Bill "Spaceman" Lee, a writer's dream who is full of off-the-wall anecdotes and still infused with the joy of baseball.

Thanks to Bill Nowlin, who taught me that writing really is 90% perspiration. And to my friend and co-author, Ben Robicheau, who reminded me that writing can also be a heck of a lot of fun.

Thanks to Moose House Publications, and especially my editor, Andrew Wetmore, who somehow manages to simultaneously shepherd several separate yet singular sets[1] of books through the labyrinth of pre-publication stages before turning them loose on the reading public; and the Art Department's Rebekah Wetmore, for the excellent cover illustration.

Thanks to my own team of editors, Glenna, Catherine, Margaret, Andy, Christine, Hal, Jan *et al*. And a preemptive thank you to the readers of *Beyond the Passage* who, despite our best efforts, will

---

1   Too much alliteration, Jim – ed.

doubtless find typos and other errors of commission or omission in this book. I beg your forgiveness.

Thanks to Linda Cann, my former editor at the Acadia *Alumni Bulletin*. Linda always loved a well-told story and valued her small stable of writers. I learned so much from her. (Who knew that 'gentile' and 'genteel' are two very different words?) And thanks to Fred Sgambati, current *Bulletin* editor, for permitting me to sharpen my writing skills on hundreds of alumni profiles about an eclectic collection of fascinating people.

And finally thanks to *Mad Magazine* for setting such an achievable standard for writers in one of their classic book reviews:

Seldom have I seen lines so equidistant from each other.

Jim Prime

About the author

Jim Prime is the author of over 20 books, mostly on the subject of sports. He co-authored *Ted Williams' Hit List* with the legendary Boston Red Sox hitter and *How Hockey Explains Canada* with Canadian hockey icon Paul Henderson. He has also collaborated with baseball eccentric Bill "Spaceman" Lee on two books.

He has contributed articles to various magazines including *Baseball Digest*, *Atlantic Insight*, *Atlantic Advocate*, *The Ring*, *Boxing Illustrated*, and the *Acadia Alumni Bulletin*, where he briefly served as editor. He's a five-time winner of the People's Choice award at the Kings Shorts Festival of Ten Minute Plays in Annapolis Royal.

Jim grew up in Freeport on Long Island and will always consider himself an islander. He lives in New Minas in the Annapolis Valley with his wife, Glenna.

Printed in the USA
CPSIA information can be obtained
at www.ICGtesting.com
LVHW011052241023
761968LV00018B/889